Walking With the Green Man

Walking With the Green Man

Father of the Forest, Spirit of Nature

By Dr. Bob Curran

Illustrated by Ian Daniels

New Page Books
A Division of The Career Press, Inc.
Franklin Lakes, NJ

WALKING WITH THE GREEN MAN
EDITED AND TYPESET BY GINA TALUCCI
Cover design by Jeff Piasky, New Page Books Production Department
Cover and interior art by Ian Daniels
Printed in the U.S.A. by Book-mart Press

To order this title, please call toll-free 1-800-CAREER-1 (NJ and Canada: 201-848-0310) to order using VISA or MasterCard, or for further information on books from Career Press.

The Career Press, Inc., 3 Tice Road, PO Box 687,
Franklin Lakes, NJ 07417
www.careerpress.com
www.newpagebooks.com

Library of Congress Cataloging-in-Publication Data

Curran, Bob.
    Walking with the green man : father of the forest, spirit of nature / by Bob Curran.
        p. cm.
    Includes bibliographical references and index.
    ISBN-13: 978-156414-931-2
    ISBN-10: 1-56414-931-5
        1. Green Man (Tale) 2. Human-plant relationships. 3. Philosophy of nature. 4. Human beings—Effect of environment on. I. Title.

GR75.G64W35 2007
398′.368216--dc22

                                                                2006038033

Dedication

To my wife, Mary, and to my children, Michael and Jennifer, for all their patience and forbearance throughout the writing of this book. And to Michael Pye, Adam Schwartz, Gina Talucci, and all the staff at New Page Books for their help, encouragement, and support.

Contents

Introduction

Shadows in the Sunlight

If you were to go to the post office on High Street in the small town of Steyning in Sussex, England and look upwards, you might see a rather curiously carved roof-beam. It is carved in the shape of a wooden head with branches starting from its cheeks and foliage around its mouth. This carving, it is said, was once the centerpiece of a timber-frame building— the Swan Inn—that stood on the site, centuries before the post office existed. Locally, the carving is known as "Jack in the Green," and it is certainly very striking, but not unique.

In the gatehouse of Battle Abbey, in the same county, similar carvings look down from an archway that was reputedly constructed in the 13th century. These are known locally as "Green Men," a variant of the Jack in the Green. This is not the only church in which these foliate heads (and sometimes naked figures surrounded by foliage) appear, for they are carved in various ancient places of worship all across England. Indeed, they even appear in Scotland and Wales

Foliate head

as far north as Orkney, where three stone heads, all sprouting foliage, appear in the north and south aisles of St. Magnus's Cathedral in Kirkwall; one head is seen disgorging carved lizards from its mouth. Again, the Jack in the Green or Green Man appears in places of public importance, such as the Committee Room in the Guildhall in

York while two other foliate heads appear in ornamentation in the main hall. In such austere buildings, the representation of the foliate head assumes a certain immediacy and importance.

So what do these strange carved heads adorning inns, churches, and public buildings mean? Why are they there? And what is their special significance, as they adorn both pub signs and cathedrals? Who was Jack in the Green? And though he is certainly a highlight in England and in English architecture, does he appear (or even perhaps have his origins in) other cultures across the world? Clearly the idea of a human head disgorging foliage (and sometimes animals) is a very ancient one that certainly goes back into distant antiquity, perhaps even to the very roots of Mankind itself. In many respects, the image seems to be imbedded within the psyche of early Man himself. Perhaps it is an iconic symbol denoting Man's position with regard to the world around him and how he once saw himself within it. Maybe it is a physical representation of Man set within the Natural environment from which he now feels himself estranged.

But the idea of the Green Man or Jack in the Green is much wider than a simple foliate head appearing on a sign outside a hostelry or on the pew ends, stone bosses or archways of a church. Under a number of names, such as John Barleycorn (the Lord of the Grain), the Man in the Oak, and others, he turns up time and again as the centerpiece of many old English festivals, some of which date back to a time before the Reformation. In some English villages there are still celebrations at certain times of the year, centering around a foliate figure usually termed Jack in the Green. Robin Goodfellow, the Green Man, or the Oak Man usually presides.

The presence of this figure bestows a blessing on the proceedings, legitimizes the festivities, and usually gives its name to the whole celebration (for example, the Oak Man's Fair, John Barleycorn's Fair, or Jack in the Green's Day). In all of these celebrations, the central figure is always treated with great respect, and is usually accompanied by local dancers or musicians who act as his servants. These ceremonies hint at a much earlier time and may well be the remnants of ancient celebrations from as far back as pre-Christian times. Many of these are to be found at certain specified times of the year, each one of them connected with the passing of the seasons or with some sort of natural occurrence— harvest, Midsummer, winter, and so on.

It is suggested, therefore, that both the figure around which the celebration is centered and the celebration itself may serve to mark some connection between Mankind and the Natural forces that surround it. Unfortunately, with the advance of modern technology, many of them are now dying out. But a mystery still surrounds the figure at the center of these gatherings: Who was he (or sometimes she—as in the Queen of the May), and why should people gather in his or her honor? And indeed, what is the true significance of such festivals? Are they simple communal events, or do they hold a deeper significance or resonance, stretching back to a time when England was much darker and more Pagan? Is the foliate man perhaps the last vestige of the ancient gods that once ruled the English countryside in times long before the coming of Christianity?

So far we have mentioned only England, and it is here that instances of the Green Man seem most evident (indeed when we think of the figure, we often immediately associate it with rural, medieval England), but is he specific solely to English tradition, or are there instances of him in other cultures as well? Can traces of similar or comparable foliate figures be found in, say, Middle and Far Eastern mythology, legend, and folklore? If, as is suspected, the Green Man serves as a cultural connection between Man and Nature, are there

The Keeper

also traces of this connection in the traditions of other peoples besides the English? The answer may be a surprising one.

Lastly, as already noted, many of the images of the Green Man appear within religious precincts (usually in Christian churches in England, Wales, and Scotland). But in many cases, the formal Church authorities took a rather dim (or at least an ambivalent) view of the ancient idea—to them it smacked of Paganism and of strange and blasphemous gods. Conventional Christianity railed against such an idea—particularly the idea of the village festivals centered around an ancient figure—so much so that during the English Reformation, when religious fervor gripped the land, many of these festivals disappeared.

And yet, as we shall see, aspects of the Christian message may have had their roots in the original Green Man tradition—especially the idea of resurrection. Is it because of this connection, perhaps, that the Green Man figures have become a part of ecclesiastical decoration? Does such largely medieval church artwork hint at other, deeper forms of worship that have not quite been forgotten, but which lie somewhere at the back of the religious mind? Nowadays, we can argue that we glorify God through Nature, but are there other, more hidden elements in such thinking? Are these characterized by the imagery of the Green Man in the decoration within many churches? Is there a secret message concealed there?

And is there also a historical element to this figure? Through the years it may have appeared in many guises. As we shall see, there are connections to Herne the Hunter, and perhaps even to the character of Robin Hood, the famous outlaw of Sherwood Forest in England; even more so to certain Orders of military knights, such as the enigmatic Knights Templar, who reputedly brought "great secrets,"

Forest God

back from the Holy Land, and who are allegedly directly connected with the building of Rosslyn Chapel in Scotland. Much has been made of this recently, in Dan Brown's best-selling book (and the resulting film) *The Da Vinci Code*. But is the hypothesis accurate—were the Templars inextricably linked to the Green Man, or do we simply *think* they were? Does the idea of the Green Man contain, as some religious thinkers have alleged, elements of Witchcraft and sorcery, or even older and much different religions that have some-how become absorbed into the mainstream faiths.

And perhaps most intriguingly, we must ask if the Green Man has ever been a woman. Certainly there are hints and allusions to this in some of the figures that appear at the festivals and in some artwork, for example the figure of the Queen (not the King) of the May, which appeared on May Day (May 1) or the Summer Solstice.

The figure of the Green Man is an incredibly complex one, raising a whole host of questions and possibilities. There is no doubt that, as a symbol, it is a very ancient one, and indeed, some of the answers to these questions may have been lost to us over time; oth-ers may be virtually impossible to tease out. There is little doubt that the figure initially represents Nature, renewal, and reproduc-tion, and it is closely linked to the passing of the seasons (includ-ing the waxing and waning of the sun). It is the representation of the Natural world at its most verdant—the growth in the hedges, bushes, and sunlit fields. And yet, is there a much darker side to this icon—a kind of shadow moving amongst the streaming sun-light? Something dark and incredibly ancient? Something that connects us to our very roots as human beings?

If this is indeed the case, then it might explain why the icon of the Green Man has become such a powerful figure across the centuries and why it has remained intact, despite many attempts to destroy it over the years. It may, in fact, be a part of the human psychology, the way in which we perceive ourselves in relation to the world around us, and is therefore an important part of what makes us human. The image of the Green Man is therefore innately recognized as an important part of our evolutionary history as a species.

The purpose of this book is to explore the concept of the Green Man and perhaps introduce the icon to those who may not be familiar with it. A walk with the Green Man will take us to many places, and through the ages from the earliest history, to the Middle East and beyond. Familiar characters such as Robin Hood may take on unfamiliar guises, and the resonances of The *Da Vinci Code* will also be examined.

The walk will take us through medieval English fairs and celebrations and, astonishingly, the steaming jungles of New Guinea. It will take us into the very basis of ourselves and our distinct identity in the surrounding world. It will take us through Mesopotamian temples and rural English churches. It is a walk that will take us both through history and the present. It is a walk through the mythology, legend, and history that have shaped and molded us all as a people on the planet. And at its end, we may know something fundamental about ourselves. It is therefore a walk that is well worth taking.

High up on the porch of Winchester Public School in Hampshire, a carven boss of a foliate head continues to smile enigmatically down on those who pass below it. Its smile is common to many other representations of the Green Man, wherever they are found—a strange, knowing smile that seems to suggest a hidden knowledge that it might be unwilling to share, and that might be beyond the imaginations of most humans. It is suggestive of a wisdom that is as old as time. So let's take a walk with the Green Man and see if we can glimpse a portion of that knowledge which is emblematic of the mysterious figure and yet, at the same time, is a part of us all.

Chapter 1

The Thing in the Forest

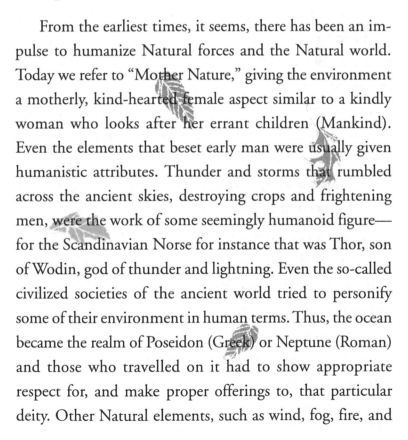

From the earliest times, it seems, there has been an impulse to humanize Natural forces and the Natural world. Today we refer to "Mother Nature," giving the environment a motherly, kind-hearted female aspect similar to a kindly woman who looks after her errant children (Mankind). Even the elements that beset early man were usually given humanistic attributes. Thunder and storms that rumbled across the ancient skies, destroying crops and frightening men, were the work of some seemingly humanoid figure— for the Scandinavian Norse for instance that was Thor, son of Wodin, god of thunder and lightning. Even the so-called civilized societies of the ancient world tried to personify some of their environment in human terms. Thus, the ocean became the realm of Poseidon (Greek) or Neptune (Roman) and those who travelled on it had to show appropriate respect for, and make proper offerings to, that particular deity. Other Natural elements, such as wind, fog, fire, and so on took on human aspects—the world fairly teemed with river gods and mountain deities. And with this personalization there also came a sense of separateness—the deity was somehow separate from the worshipper and could be conversed with, appealed to, or placated. The Natural forces somehow seemed to lie outside humanity and were distinct from it.

This was probably not always the case. The emergence of a distinct, human identity, set apart from the forces of the Natural world, probably evolved over a period of time. We are, of course, unable to establish when the split between Mankind and the rest of Nature actually occurred, but at one time Man must have considered himself to be a part of the Natural world, existing in and perceiving the world just as any other animal might. Of course, Creationists will no doubt argue with such a concept, citing that Man emerged in the world fully formed and with a distinct consciousness all of his own; however, more recognized scientific theories seem to bear this out. We know, for example, that there were several species of men (and there may have been even more than we suspect) who viewed the world in different ways. We also know that originally Man was a hunter who competed with other animals for food.

The consciousness and perceptions of these early men (or as some have described them, quasi-men) may well have been very different from our own. They may have viewed the world in terms of hunting and prey, and may have perceived themselves as part of that dichotomy. They ate, probably performed sexual acts without too much thought, killed, slept, and hunted, largely by instinct. When they hunted, they probably travelled in packs or groups, as some other animals did. Their consciousness was a part of the Natural world. All the same, they were something rather special, for they had within them the power of evolution.

This "Natural consciousness" did not mean that they were unaware of external forces. The early world was certainly shaken by storms, earthquakes, floods, and other dangers. However, it is unclear how these were perceived by the rudimentary mind. They were probably seen in the same way that other animals viewed such events. But as the species evolved, other perceptions took hold. Indeed, for Homo sapiens such notions began to emerge slightly later than they did for other species of men. We know, for example, that Neanderthal Man probably buried his dead before our own ancestors started to (Homo sapiens simply abandoned their dead as meat for scavengers or ate it themselves), hinting at something that might lie *outside* the immediate sphere of existence.

And with evolution, the perception of the species changed. Neanderthal Men died out and it was left to the more aggressive Homo sapiens to evolve into our ancestors, and to take on new perceptions of the world around them. The idea of *separateness* and the notion of something that lay *beyond* the present was beginning to take hold. The elements were still there—there were still storms, earthquakes, and floods—but these were gradually taking on a new significance as the human consciousness developed. They were certainly still to be feared—that was the basic instinct of the animal— but perhaps they were controlled and could *be* controlled.

This idea arose out of a fundamental shift in the humans' perception of themselves. Previously, they had competed with other animals for food and resources but they had competed as *equals*. When it came to hunting, they perceived themselves as similar to the wolf and the bear with whom they fought for available meat. Evolution changed all that. As the human brain grew, together with Mankind's knowledge and skills, a sense of separateness from the Natural world began to enter human thinking. Hunting was no longer conducted by instinct, but by strategy; Homo sapiens noticed that bears, wolves, and wild pigs were less able to control and organize their world than they were. With a newfound cognizance, they were able to plan ahead and work out ways in which they could actually trap their prey rather than simply relying on chasing it down. They were now far better—in their own eyes at least—than other animals that could not. Concomitant with this was a growing sense of individuality, as certain members of the herd began to develop new strategies and methods of organization due to their unique skills, which each one of them held. Suddenly, rather than being a part of the Natural world, the environment became something *distinct* and something they might be able to control. And if *they* were able to control their world, other entities might be able to do so as well.

Because, although they could lay traps for their prey, the Natural elements still terrified them. There were storms, eruptions, earthquakes, and great windstorms for which there seemed to be no rhyme or reason. For small clans of humans living upon the edge of subsistence, life was precarious. A sudden flood or a drought could destroy their entire world; a powerful storm could perhaps sweep it away, killing them all. At times too, their prey was plentiful and everyone was well-fed, but at other times there was nothing at all. Why was that? Why could there not be meat available when they wanted it? If *they* could control the world, then perhaps something else could too. The notion of powers and intelligences *outside* and separate from themselves was starting to emerge.

The first ideas of these powers were of vague, nebulous beings. The early Semites, for instance, viewed their gods as windstorms or as cloudy pillars, glimpsed either early in the morning or late in the evening. Some other ancient peoples simply worshipped the sun, which was visible throughout the day, or the moon at night. Other parts of the Natural world were worshipped too—for the early Celts, for instance, spirits were everywhere: within stones, trees, rivers, lakes, and wells. They watched Mankind with curious, if not sometimes hostile eyes and were responsible for all the benefits and calamities that befell their human neighbors. In other cases, animals, with whom Men had once competed for resources and food, were often worshipped for qualities that their devotees admired—the bull for strength, the horse for swiftness, the wolf for cunning, and the bear for bravery. What was important, however, was that these forces were *out there* and were distinct from Humankind and the skills it had.

And yet, there was a memory of the time when Men had actually been an equal part of the Natural world. There was a "stream of consciousness," which lay almost dormant in the human brain and connected our ancestors with the world outside themselves in a very fundamental way. This is what psychoanalysts such as Carl Jung have identified as the psyche—a great body of consciousness to which we have no immediate access that displays elements of both the individual and the collective. This is where the "I," the ego, is defined, but it is defined *in relation to* the collective—the human is defined as a consciousness *beyond* that of its environment, but is given its definition *by* that environment.

Thus, there was an imperative goal amongst early Men to shape and define that environment into an image they could understand, and in terms they could easily recognize. In this way, the forces of Nature could perhaps be controlled and mediated. Rather than being disparate energies that roamed aimlessly through the countryside or that crackled across the skies, they would be given a form and purpose. In that way they could be appealed to, invoked, or commanded by Mankind. Here lay the origins of both magic and religion. By making these forces recognizable, humans also made it possible to interact with them in a recognizable way. Thus, the disembodied spirits and deities began to take on physical characteristics—put in crude terms, they often took on a *face*. Sometimes, they also took on bodies as well, such as in early cave paintings, perhaps designed to invoke some hunting spirit to ensure success in the hunt. But as Mankind evolved, so the idea of the controlling agencies— the gods—became more complex. They appeared more recognizable in a physical sense and began to display human behavioral characteristics. They were angry, they were petulant, they were capricious, they were crafty, they suffered the pangs of jealousy, they enjoyed a joke, they were drunken. By the time of the great Mediterranean civilizations—Greek and Roman—the gods had become something of an exclusive club, dwelling away in the high mountains and interfering in the affairs of humans often merely for amusement, sport, or for some form of self-gratification. For the most part, they were human in both form and temperament. The personalization of these deities made them both more accessible and more immediate. They also refined the systems of worship—for example, how could a god actually *hear* a devotee's supplication if he or she had no ears; how could he or she *see* the supplicant if there were no eyes? How could he or she receive offerings without hands? This humanization of the deity continued in the Christian West well into the 20th century. Many Christians saw God as an old man, a patriarch, who kept a constant watch over the world, perhaps from a cloud high in Heaven. At the time, deities had become largely humanized.

But this is not the whole story, because somewhere, locked away at the back of the human mind, was that basic connection with Nature, which Man had experienced in his earliest days. It found its expression amongst some of the lesser or more lowly regarded deities and in connections between gods and Nature. Satyrs for example embodied nature and Natural behavior, while the satyr-god Bacchus often epitomized drunkenness, hedonism, and earthly pleasures. The Bacchanalia, the great feast in his honor, was one of excess and license, in which humans often emulated the behavior of animals. The portrayal of both satyrs and of Bacchus depicted them as creatures with human torsos and heads, but with the hindlegs of a goat—in effect a merger of both human being and animal. They were earthy, bawdy beings that enjoyed sexuality to excess. This equated well with the ancient deities who were associated with fertility and reproduction, but they also forged a linkage between both the human and Natural worlds. They would later appear as timid fauns—still half man, half goat—to be made famous by Mr. Tumnus in C.S. Lewis's *The Lion, the Witch and the Wardrobe*, which formed the basis for the recent film *The Chronicles of Narnia*. Similarly, entities in Greek Thessaly displayed the characteristics of both humans and horses. These were the centaurs that sported the upper torso of a man and the lower body of a horse, and could travel as fast as the wind. Although the idea may have grown out of the swift horsemen

A Bacchanalia

who came from the region, there seems to be little doubt that this was a notion that had grown out of the connection between men and nature. And they were not alone: the Greek Poseidon, god of the sea, is often represented in art as having the tail of a fish or the elongated lower body of an eel. The gods, it seemed, had not all completely developed human characteristics, and some vestiges of the ancient animal/Natural world still remained.

This perception probably stretched back to the developing individuality of early man when he looked beyond the centrality of his campsite towards the dark, gloomy, and threatening forest beyond the comforting circle of light from his fire. Out there were *things*, which could hurt him or destroy him, but they were beings that were *distinct* from him and possibly more powerful than he. There were animals of course, but there might be other beings too— the physical manifestations of forces and Natural energies. They had their own agendas that were vastly different from his. He was no longer part of their world.

The most potent symbol, however, is to be found in the Book of Genesis in the Christian Bible. In the original story, told in the first few chapters, Adam and Eve dwell in an earthly paradise known as the Garden of Eden. They are happy there and at one with nature—they are naked but are not conscious of it. They may enjoy all earthly pleasures, says their Creator God, except to eat from the Tree of Knowledge in the center of the Garden. Tempted by the serpent (an ancient symbol of evil), however, they eat from the Tree and suddenly realize that they are naked—that is, that they are no longer part of the Natural world. They now have a greater knowledge than the animals around them, but because they disobeyed God, they are cast out of the Garden. They now have to fend for themselves in the wider world. Despite his disobedience, Adam still retains an initial "mastery over the beasts of the field" that God has given him.

This metaphor of a lost connection with Nature is both simple and striking. Adam and Eve (read man and woman) existed on an instinctive level but in harmony with the Natural world around them. As they evolved, however, they gain "knowledge," acknowledged their "nakedness" (therefore, they were not as the animals around them), and were "ashamed" of their primitive state. They cover themselves and leave the earthly paradise of the Garden of Eden, to act as individuals in the world, and separate from nature. The collective unity with the Natural world has been severed.

The Archtype

The Genesis story is unquestionably an early Semitic myth concerning Creation and the origins of the human condition, but it is also a mechanism of explaining and dealing with the separation between Men and Nature. The Green Man is another such mechanism. The humanoid face that peers from amongst the leaves, or the foliage-covered figure that lurks deep in the forest, serves as a symbol of that former union that has now been lost. The face that looks out on the world is that of a recognizable human, not that of an animal or some alien being. It is the representation of humanity, swathed and clothed in the Natural world. And similar to the Genesis story, it portrays Man at one with the living environment around him. It might be described as an archetype—an image denoting that great untapped consciousness within us, both individually and collectively, of which we are vaguely aware but cannot really articulate in fully coherent terms. It is the humanizing of that "stream of consciousness," so to speak, from an analogue (continuous) language into a more digitalized, tangible form. It is the humanness of the face, set amongst growth that links Mankind to the Natural world around us.

A Closer Look

A word also needs to be said about the face itself. It seems invariably to be a masculine countenance, sometimes (though not always) adorned by a beard, which was the symbol of sagacity, power, and authority in the ancient world. It also symbolized recklessness or a Devil-may-care attitude, for a beard was also a hazardous thing to sport during a battle: In hand-to-hand combat, an opponent could grab the warrior's beard (if it were long enough) and hold him until a fatal blow to the head was delivered. So in some cases, rather than denoting sagacity, the beard denoted a more capricious nature, fitting in with the often whimsical and unpredictable Nature of the environment.

Some representations of the Green Man, of course, have no beard at all and often display a kind of bisexual nature. This raises an important question. Although we speak of the Green *Man* and ascribe to him a long mythological pedigree, should we assume that the earliest gods—as perhaps represented by the figure—are in fact *male?*

Much of the evidence that we have appears to suggest that the earliest deities were *female.* While we know that hunting gods (who seem to have been exclusively male) were worshipped in earliest times (female hunting entities would be venerated later), one of the earliest concerns amongst ancient peoples was the idea of birth and repro-duction, which was solely a female activity. Amongst the early Celts, for example, the ability to give birth seems to have been highly ven-erated. We can deduce this from peculiar and very ancient small stone figures that turn up in a number of sites (some of them mon-asteries and churches) all over Ireland, Scotland, England, and Wales, and in some parts of Europe, such as Austria and southern Russia. These are known as Sheela- (Sheelagh or Sile) -na-gigs. These are minute depictions of a nude female figure, her face often either indistinct or monstrous, but with heavy, pendulous, milk-filled breasts and a swollen stomach. In most instances she is crouching down, opening or holding open an enormous vulva in what clearly seems to be a sexual invitation. The name of the figure is rather ambigu-ous. It is usually taken as deriving from the Irish *Sile na gCioch* (Sheela of the Breasts), although it may also have its origins in *Sile na gob* (Sheela on her hunkers—displaying her vagina).

Both of these are clear reference to the sexual nature of the fig-ure and its connections with birth and child-rearing. In his book *Encyclopaedia of Sacred Sexuality* however, Rufus Camphausen sug-gests that the name may have Middle Eastern origins, and points out that the original phraseology may have contained the ancient Mesopotamian "nu gug," which means "pure and immaculate." Whatever her origins, the Sheela-na-gig belongs to a type of ico-nography known as "Willendorf women" (from the area of Willendorf in Austria where such statuettes were first found), which are probably amongst the oldest depictions of women that we have. However, the age of many of these Sheelas is not known—most of them appear to come from a much later date than the earliest civili-zations. Some appear in the walls, gateposts, or churches of medi-

eval towns, and it is possible that some were even carved then, maybe
even as late as 1100, so the actual antiquity of such figures is often
called into question. They may not have been early prehistoric deities, although they are concerned with reproduction and sex, which
were prominent themes in prehistoric life. Even the later figures
may demonstrate a memory that was still current in the early medieval period.

Why the Female Archetype?

But the Sheela-na-gig was not just regarded as an image of female sexuality. In some areas, she was regarded as the symbol of
nurturing, prosperity, and protection—common female attributes.
For example, a Sheela appears in the main gateway to the town of
Fethard, in County Tipperary, Southern Ireland, where some regard her as the protector of the town. She is actually set into the
medieval bridge over the Glashawley River, which at one time was
the town's main thoroughfare. For many years at Seir Keiron—an
incredibly old Christian monastic site in South Offaly, Ireland, possibly dating from A.D. 401—a Sheela-na-gig was placed in the church
wall where it was widely regarded as a symbol of good luck. It was
removed at the end of the 1800s or beginning of the 1900s after a
local Anglican clergyman objected to its blatant sexuality so close to
a holy building, and was taken to the National Museum in Dublin.
There are also many more scattered throughout Ireland; at one time
it was thought that many of them were scattered across the North of
Ireland, but that these were destroyed as Pagan relics during the
Protestant Reformation there. The same is suggested to have hap-
pened in some parts of England as well.

It was originally thought that Sheela-na-gigs had been brought into and placed in churches, convents, and monasteries to take away their evil, Pagan influence. However, the reasons for them appearing in such places may be slightly more complex than that. Indeed, some of them may have been specifically carved for holy houses, particularly during the medieval period. There was a very old belief amongst many peoples that a human sexual figure prominently displayed might turn away evil spirits and demons, so some of the Sheela-na-gigs may well have been employed to protect the holy ground from evil forces—an idea that we will be looking at later in this book. Perhaps the Sheela also acted as a link between the old nature worship of the past and the formal Christianity of the medieval time (when the old beliefs had not quite died out). It remained as a symbol for those who still found devout Christianity difficult to deal with.

This is not to say that their inclusion within holy precincts went unopposed. In France, the strict St. Bernard of Clairvaux riled against the shamelessness of such imagery within sacred places, which often distracted the faithful from their books and holy study. In England too, St. Coelfrid, abbot of the monastery of St. Peter and St. Paul in Kent, raged against images that inspired "lewd thoughts" within the minds of the monks at his Abbey. This, he agued, made the faithful behave in "unseemly ways." He was presumably not the only holy abbot to feel this way.

The Falling Away of Sexuality

At some time, perhaps during the early medieval period or maybe even earlier, the idea of the woman with the swollen belly, great breasts, and gaping vagina seems to have given way to a more male-orientated figure. The notion of sexuality, however, still seems to have been paramount. In the medieval church at Artun in Burgundy, France, a naked male carving displays both his anus and testicles in what might be considered by some to be an obscene show. In some other French churches, a male figure is seen with an erect penis. These images may, once again, be devices to drive away dark spirits, or they may provide a link with the earthy, rustic religions that preceded Christianity in those areas. It may also be a logical male interpretation of the female goddess, sometimes known as the Earth Mother. And if we once more follow the line logically, we will probably arrive at a male figure who does not show his genitals or his anus (a definite snub to invading demons), but who rather peers out from amid the foliage, symbolizing the relatively primitive and untamed world. Although it maintains the connection between man and nature, it is, of course, a much more subtle image than the man waving his penis or showing his backside, and perhaps much more in keeping with the holy precincts of the site around it. Such an overtly sexual image was now replaced by a human face or figure peering discreetly through the leaves or from behind some foliage. Whether it would have satisfied the likes of Bernard of Clairvaux or St. Coelfrid and his clerical contemporaries is another matter entirely.

The Monarch

The Green Man, however, is more than just an ornamental carving to be found in medieval churches, monasteries, or city gates—it is often a character in a ritual folk festival. It is not always called the Green Man but sometimes appears as the King of the Wood or (in its female form) the Queen of the May. Yet even here, its origins and purpose lie in the Natural world. In some folk plays and ritualized dramas, the Green Man is a monarch that dies, only to rise again and rule in splendor once more. The connection with nature in the wintertime is obvious: The natural foliage goes into decay in autumn, perishes in the winter frosts, but rises again to flourish in spring and summer. There may have been many of these rituals at one time, but changes in religious and political emphasis (for example, the rise of Puritanism in, say, England) extinguished them once and for all, and they are now lost to us. Nevertheless, some old folk traditions still remain in scattered areas of the Celtic world, largely in parts of England. For instance, in Hastings, Jack in the Green appears as a rather gigantic figure, a man in a framework, decked with foliage (usually laurel), carried by a man. He is sometimes accompanied by "Black Sal" (or Black Sally, who may represent his female element, harking back to the ancient, ancestral goddesses of the prehistoric world). During a pageant, Jack is ritually killed; this releases the "spirit of summer or Nature" when the festivities can truly begin. This is also a remembrance of what is sometime referred to as the "old ways," that fundamental knowledge about ourselves and the world around us that had been handed down from former times—the death of winter and the flowering of Nature once more—the very message conveyed by the image of the Green Man.

According to Sir James Frazer in his seminal book on folklore and anthropology, *The Golden Bough* (published in 1922), the King of the Wood was both a monarch and a priest. More, he was both the embodiment and protector of Nature. Amongst many ancient peoples including the Celts, the monarch was the physical manifestation of the

forces that held Nature together. In places all over the world, such
as Ireland and Scotland, the King was required to place his right
foot in a specially carved footprint to symbolize his union with the
earth. Many of these are to be found all over the Irish and Scottish
countryside where they are often attributed by the later Christians
to saints and holy men. In one case, at the ancient Skerry Church
near the holy mountain of Slemish in North Antrim, Northern
Ireland, the footprint is attributed to the angel Victor who reputedly gave St. Patrick his mission in Ireland, and also handed him his
holy staff or crozier, the *Beculum Jesu*. Despite such holy legends,
the location of the church—sited on a hill, which looks down the
entire Maine Valley as far as Antrim, suggests that the place was
originally an inauguration site where ancient kings made their union
with the earth in a public manner. At a number of churches too,
there are large stones with indentations on them where prehistoric
kings probably prostrated themselves during their inauguration in
a kind of sexual act with the earth—these are now more discreetly
described as "saint's stones" where Christian saints allegedly prayed.
At Dunadd, in the Kilmartin Valley in Scotland, a great double-
ringed earthworks is suggestive of another such site. Here, the monarch rose up from behind one of the earthen walls as though
emerging from the ground itself. Such inaugurations may have been
done at night and by torchlight to give a greater dramatic effect.
The message was the same—the monarch was somehow inextricably connected with the earth over which he or she ruled. Indeed,
everything that went either right or wrong in the Natural world
was, in the eyes of their subjects, connected to the monarch.

Thus, if there was a drought or a flood, or if the projected crops
didn't appear, the fault lay with the king. For example, several

ancient Irish texts describe a great rainstorm that flattened many of
the crops in Ulster in the 3rd century. This was ascribed to the King
of Ulster whipping his horses in a certain spot, offending the gods
of nature. He was placed under a *gaesa* (a supernatural and ritualized act of contrition or atonement) by the Druids, and after he had
fulfilled this, harmony was restored and there were no further storms.
Furthermore, no monarch could rule if he had a bodily blemish
because that might transfer itself into the natural environment (he
was the *embodiment* of that environment after all) and harm his
people in some way. The famous Irish king, Conn of the Hundred
Battles, is alleged to have relinquished the High Kingship of Ireland
after losing an eye in battle lest his disfigurement should transfer
itself into the world around him.

With the onset of advancing years, many monarchs grew more
feeble and began to physically deteriorate. There was a fear that this
steady deterioration, with the onset of old age, would be reflected
in the world about. Therefore, in accordance with natural laws, the
monarch had to die and be replaced by a young and invigorated
one who would restore the natural balance. This was, as James Frazer
states, the death of the King of the Wood and the emergence of a
new regime. The character of the Green Man within folk tradition
may reflect this, as he too is ritually slain in many folk pageants, only
to rise up again to reign once more.

This idea of the restoration of the monarch, coupled with the
restoration of Nature, allows the Green Man to be known by many
other names—the Garland King for example (he is hung with garlands, representing the Natural world over which he also presides),
the Green Knight (at which we shall look slightly later in this book),
Old Winter, and so on, all representing death and resurrection.

This, of course, fit in well with the Christian message. Akin to the King of the Wood, *Christ* had also died and risen again and continued to reign in Heaven. Therefore, the symbol of the Green Man could even be incorporated into some of the Christian pageants within the early Church.

Throughout history, the Green Man has appeared in various tableaux across the Western Christian world. He has appeared as the legendary figure King Arthur (accompanied by his female aspect, Queen Guenevere), as King Brute (or Brutus—a legendary Roman ruler of England), as the Summer King (accompanied by his consort, the Summer Queen), or Jack in the Green (purportedly an old and mysterious medieval entity). In some parts of England (for example, in Castleton in Derbyshire), the figure is associated with the restoration of the monarchy of Charles II in 1660, after the period of the Puritan Commonwealth. The symbolism here is obvious and stretches well beyond political concerns. The festival appears to date from the 18th century, but it is clearly much older than that. Always at the center of the play and usually the subsequent procession is the figure of the Green Man (or some other alias), and much of the festivities revolve around it. And there was perhaps another symbolism contained in the figure, especially around May Day—one that was once again strongly connected with sexuality.

Rites of Passage and Revelry

For many young people, young men especially, the May Day celebrations were supposedly a rite of passage from childhood to adulthood. With the bursting forth of Nature, it was a time when girls became women, boys became men, and they would both take partners. Many of the rituals that were celebrated around this time concerned the death of childhood and the procession into adulthood. Boys and girls are therefore "reborn" as adult, sexual beings; this process of transition was often presided over by the King of the Wood, Jack in the Green, or some other such entity—all possible variants, it would seem, of the Green Man. The figure "bestows" a sexual awakening on each boy and each girl and prepares them to go into the world as grown-ups. Their childhood is "dead" and a new life is reborn.

This was also a time when young men ceased to depend upon their families and became warriors in their own right—another rite of death and rebirth. Here, the King "bestowed" ingenuity, skill, and strength to each boy, making him into a hunter or fighter. In some instances, the transition entailed leaving the shelter and security of the village or family and going off alone into the wild, natural world. This might sometimes be done at the behest of the King of the Wood or Green Man. An interpretation of this may suggest a reunion with Nature, and a return to the earlier times when Man felt much closer to his environment, and indeed, was an integral part of it. Thus, the Nature figure was a key image in the "coming of age" for many young people and symbolic of the transition between youth and maturity.

In its complete form, the image of the Green Man is also associated with revelry and dancing. This is closely linked with the ceremonies described previously. In many cases, such revelries were closely connected with the disappearance of winter and the celebrations that followed it. In the midst of the festivities, a figure appeared trailing green to preside over the fun and frolic. This was a time when inhibitions were laid aside and sexual symbolism took precedence. The most common symbol associated with this is the May Pole, the phallic imagery of which is obvious; the ceremony was held on May 1 when the last effects of winter were thought to have finally disappeared. Curiously, May Day in the British Isles is the only overtly Pagan festival not to have a Christian saint latterly associated with it. In England, the act of young maidens dancing around the May Pole can be traced back to the late 1400s and early 1500s, although the tradition is certainly far older than that. Indeed, there are references to "the May Games" to be found in manuscripts such as *The Chronicles of Britain* written by an unnamed monk around 1150 and in Geoffrey of Monmouth's *History of the Kings of Britain* written in 1130. It is almost certain that these Games also included some form of ritualized festival. The Pole itself is erect and is traditionally made of oak or some other hardy wood. Around this young girls danced, possibly attaching themselves directly to the May Pole by holding on to ribbons or rope. Strong drink was readily available and indeed one of the names given to the Green Man during these revelries is "John Barleycorn," the spirit of whiskey and other forms of alcohol, sometimes known as "King of the Corn" or the "King of the Barley" (the compound description giving him his familiar name). In some of the festivals, he would appear in a green coat, waving what was alleged to be a bottle of home-produced spirits, grabbing at young girls in a parody of drunken lust. The whole tableau was meant to be one of fun and frolic, but perhaps the Pagan ritualistic undertones were obvious.

It is not surprising then that the Christian Church opposed such revelry—sometimes in the most vehement form. In England, during the period of the Commonwealth (1649–1660) for instance,

such revelries were conducted under pain of death for the participants. For example, the Puritan Parliament formally banned all such
merriment during the period of the English Interregnum (1649–
1659) as "Pagan sacrilege," and condemned those who participated
to Hell. In spite of this official prohibition, the revelries continued
unabated in certain isolated parts of the English countryside and even
enjoyed something of a resurgence during the reigns of Charles II
(1660–1685) and his brother James II (1685–1688) before falling
away again during the joint monarchy of William III and Mary II
(1688–1702). During its resurgence it was allegedly imbued with a
certain "Catholic" or "Popish" tinge and was frowned upon by many
English Protestants.

Around this time, the Green Man seems to have adopted something of another guise. Some of his "greenness" seems to have disappeared and he is replaced by another, slightly darker, figure.
Although he still bore the name Jack (as in Jack in the Green), he
now resembled something akin to a blacksmith or (by the early 1800s)
a chimney sweep. Although he still presided over the revels and was
still closely associated with fertility, the reasons for this change of
image may have had something to do with the changing social view
and the steady growth of Protestantism throughout England. Smiths
and the like are often associated with the darkness and flame of the
forge, and these associations may have linked Jack in the Green to
the dark, underground world where the Devil was said to dwell.
(Incidentally, in some old folktales, the Devil himself is shown as a
blacksmith-type figure). However, the smith worked with iron, a
sacred metal, and was therefore lucky, as indeed was the chimney
sweep, who in some respects remained as a symbol of fertility. At
some weddings in Western Europe, the chimney sweep is present to
ensure good luck to the union and an abundant family to the bride

and groom. Such dark, sooty characters were often considered to be powerful and otherworldly, probably with strong connections into the natural order of things. In fact, a sooty, sweep-like figure was considered to be an aspect of Robin Goodfellow, who in turn was an aspect of the Green Man.

Despite these positive aspects of the image—the reunification with nature that still seems to be inherent in all of us; the ensuring of abundant harvests and the fertility of both humans and livestock, and the overseeing of the transition from youth into adulthood—the Green Man may also have had a darker side.

The Split Between Man and Nature

As Mankind became more "civilized"—that is, drew away from the Natural world of which he had once been a part and into more urbanized and technologically managed environments—the natural world took on an uncomfortable and much more menacing aspect. Of course, it had always been dangerous. Early man, as we have already noted, competed with other predators for food and shelter. Undoubtedly the dark forests of the ancient, Natural world held many dangers and terrors for our first ancestors. They had to contend with animals such as the bear, wild boar, and wolf, amongst others, and they also had to cope with dangerous terrain, such as bogs, rocky gullies, and deep woodland. And yet somehow they dealt with them—perhaps because they were a part of that world and an integral link in the natural chain. The knowledge and individuality that characterized the more "civilized" world changed that perception in a subtle but fundamental way. Rather than being part of the natural process, Men now viewed the Natural world as being "out there," and with that change in perception came a notion of "alienness" and fear. Some have argued that as our ancestors became more "civilized," they also became "softer" and "less hardy," but perhaps this is too simplistic an explanation. Perhaps the real problem lay somewhere within the human mind-set. Rather than being enshrouding and enfolding, Nature was perceived as being implacably hostile, maybe even actively seeking to destroy Humankind when it could. It was the notion of difference (men being now somehow "different" from the Natural world) being turned into opposition. Nature was not only to be worshipped and placated, it was also to be feared.

This imminent fear took concrete form in some of the ancient entities that began to appear in earliest times, and which continued down into the medieval period. Many of these expressed, either in shape or aspect, elements of the Natural world, and all seemed to have inimical or hostile tendencies towards the world of Men. Some were giants, some were pygmies, some seemed to be made of Natural materials—rocks, trees, bushes, and foliage. It was of course reasonable to see how this belief might have come about. In poor light—for example, at twilight when many of these entities were believed to be about—shadows moved and Natural features (rocks, trees, and bushes) seemed to move of their own volition. The land that perhaps had been very familiar at midday, suddenly became alien and threatening as night drew on. Distinctions blurred and geographical features, maybe seen at a distance, seemed to change into something else—even into monstrous and dangerous beings.

Nacht Ruprecht and Schwartz Pieter

In parts of Germany, for example, a terrifying creature, supposedly made out of sticks and twigs (or dressed in a coat made from

The Hermit

such material) and called Nacht Ruprecht (Night Rupert), went about during the hours of twilight on nefarious tasks. His home was the deep forest and he was sometimes accompanied by woodland animals or by a hideous assistant known as George Oaf, a human companion traditionally regarded as being mentally retarded. The purpose of this pair was both simple and sinister. They carried the young and defenseless or the old and weak into the forest, where they were either eaten or turned into slaves for unforgiving masters. Whether Nacht Ruprecht was indeed a being made out of natural elements or a human dressed in wild clothing, he was greatly feared and was considered a deity.

Similarly, another entity known as Schwartz Pieter (Black Peter) could invoke terror amongst many isolated communities, particularly those living on the edge of forests. Similar to Nacht Ruprecht, Schwartz Pieter appeared either at night or at dusk, but instead, he carried away young girls to his lair in the deep woodlands. He was the archetypical wild man—there was no question about his humanity. However, he was also thought to have animalistic tendencies and was believed to be a cannibal. He went about wrapped in furs, portraying himself as a beast of the wilderness. This underlined "civilized Man's" fear of the wild and his abhorrence of practices, which he now considered to be "unnatural." At one time, cannibalism may well have been extremely rife amongst humans. Archaeological indications taken from prehistoric latrines and middens show human bones that have been split in order to extract the marrow. It may well have been that some members of a community eventually ended up in the communal stockpot when they died. And it may be that some cannibalistic practices may have continued down into medieval times in remote areas. Crazy hermits and

recluses may have practiced cannibalism in their isolated forest re-
treats. Thus, the wild man who may have shunned human society,
and who may well have exemplified nature in the raw, came to be
feared and took on the guise of Schwartz Pieter or Nacht Ruprecht.
Through the years, folk beliefs in both these entities and their dubious nighttime excursions continued. Other such entities too—all
with a background in Nature—were also worshipped and feared in
various locations across Western Europe.

Later, the idea of abduction by Ruprecht and Pieter was slightly
modified. They no longer carried off the young, the old, and the
defenseless, but rather the greatest scholar, the strongest man, or
the most beautiful girl in the community for some unspecified purpose. Belief was also extended to certain other entities and even to
historical figures. For example, in Ireland, the legendary Donn Bin
Maguire, in County Fermanagh, carried off such people using a
fairy horse, to his lightless underground world beneath Binoughlin
Mountain; while in County Limerick, Gerald, the 13th Earl of
Desmond, swept away great thinkers and beautiful maidens to his
home beneath a lake. And there were many others too.

Ironically, Nacht Ruprecht and Schwartz Pieter were also gift
givers, rewarding those who worshipped them (and possibly thereby
showing the duality of the Natural order). They would lay the folkloric foundations for another, rather different, figure—the jolly old
Santa Claus. Indeed, in many early depictions of him, Santa is
wreathed in green garlands, suggestive of the Green Man and plainly
displaying his partial connection with some of the wild, old, woodland deities. Many of these dangerous forest entities and ancient
woodland gods, however, coalesced into the image of the Green
Man. This then became an amorphous figure combining all that

was good, but also, as the Christian church would later point out, containing a darker side rooted in these ancient Pagan entities.

Creatures in the Forest

Moreover, there were supposed to be monstrous creatures in the depths of the forest—things that were not quite substance and not quite shadow. In parts of Brittany, especially in the La Chatre region, for example, a creature known as *La Grand Bissetre* howled mournfully between the woodland trees on certain nights of the year. Folkloric descriptions of this creature vary but it was supposed to be man-like in shape, though rather insubstantial, wafting along woodland trails where it had a special affinity with wood and water. Its cry resembled that of a young owl and was a dreadful thing to hear, because it meant imminent death for the hearer. In many folktales, La Grand Bissetre might well be regarded as a darker aspect of Nature and of the Green Man. In both Ireland and Scotland too, a similar figure known as the *dealan-de* haunted the mountains and forests, frightening everyone with its high-pitched wailing cry. Somewhere between a fallen angel and a banshee, the dealan-de was also widely believed to be a spirit of Nature who lured inquisitive people, drawn by its strange cry, to their deaths in the woodland depths. Similar to La Grand Bissetre it was vaguely man-like in form but significantly boasted a huge and monstrous head. Creatures such as these—and there were many more scattered throughout the Celtic folklore world—were possibly potent folk memories of ancient Natural deities, and may well have had their origins in the notion of the Green Man.

The Green Man's Iconic Appearance

The color green is also significant. It is the color of spring when new life is bursting forth; it is the color of growth and vitality; It Is usually the natural color of foliage and vegetation; it is the color of the organic world. In widespread thinking, it certainly symbolizes both birth and vigor, and many scholars have characterized the Green Man as the symbol of renewal and vitality. That is certainly true. But green can also represent death, decay, and decomposition. Rather than being indicative of vitality, it is suggestive of putrescence and neglect. We speak about old metal being "green with verdigris," suggestive of age and deterioration, and in the organic world, we speak of something being "green with mold." Stagnant water is "green with scum," suggesting lifelessness and degeneration. So the color holds a twofold meaning—the bursting forth of life and the onset of decay and decomposition—which is once again reflected in the idea of the Green Man.

In the Natural world, green is also the color of concealment. The face of the Green Man is usually portrayed as looking out from amongst leaves or other foliage as though it were furtively checking to see if anyone were about. It often appears secretive in its demeanor, as though it were the face of someone who didn't want to be found. Of course, green was supposedly used by other beings or entities to conceal themselves within the natural environment and well away from human eyes. In Ireland, for example, leprechauns are often described as "little green men," or as being dressed in green in order to blend in with the background and so conceal themselves. Ancient entities too were sometimes described as "green," and were supposedly indistinguishable from their surroundings. They were certainly there but could not be physically seen. Nevertheless, their presence was impressive.

Portraying the Green Man

Although the Green Man is sometimes represented as a whole figure partially concealed amongst the woodland foliage, the image is usually portrayed simply as a head; this too is significant. Today we tend to think that the essence of people lies within their heart—the main engine of their body. From early modern times, we find expressions such as "stout-hearted," "good-hearted," "braveheart," or a "heart like a lion." However, for ancient peoples this was not where the essence of humanity was contained. They believed that the very center of the human being was the head—in fact some people (particularly early Christians) thought that this was where the soul of the person actually resided. The head contained the strength, the knowledge, and the skills of an individual; in effect it *was* the person. Thus, the ancient Celts, in common with many other races, venerated the heads of great men or famous warriors while ignoring the rest of the body, and often placed the decaying craniums on display at a well. From this came the famous Celtic idea of a headwell, or shrine where they could be touched and perhaps transfer some of their powers to others. In this way it seemed that the warrior or hero was still alive or at least in evidence and in communication with his people. The head could perhaps speak, giving out prophesies concerning the locality, offer advice, or bestow powers to those who venerated it. It was therefore appropriate that the potency of the Green Man should be represented by a head because this paralleled ancient beliefs.

Later, the Christian Church, appalled at this particularly large Pagan reference (that is, the notion of the powerful head from which all forms of evil might emanate) would seek to add a body to it, but the notion of the head prevailed (probably because the Christians also balked at the notion of nudity—as in the Sheela-na-gigs), and even became part of the Christian iconography in many churches.

The notion of the head also held other connotations, one of which was not lost on the early Christians—the idea of the mask. This brought in ancient Pagan ideas of concealment and power. We have already noted how the color green was one of concealment and, in prehistoric societies, a mask of that colour may well have hidden the face of the Shaman as he performed his magics and communicated with the forest deities. In fact, it was probably an integral part of the Pagan ritual. The early masks may well have been made from leaves or Natural materials, and provided a concealed place behind which the Shaman might observe what was going on around him. Also, when the Shaman donned his mask, he or she became someone or *something* else. He or she might become the wild creature of the forest—the connection with Nature that was reassuring and yet terrifying at the same time. Echoes of the leaf or ferny mask can still be seen in the concealing foliage that wraps itself around some of the faces.

For many Godly people, the idea of the mask also represented the concealment of evil—the smiling but false face that the Devil hid behind in order to perform his mischief. God's children, the religious and the righteous, had no need to conceal themselves, because God's glory shone through their faces. So by taking on the aspect of a mask, the face of the Green Man assumed a slightly more dubious, more sinister, interpretation.

A Shaman's mask

The Morris Men

There were some further implications in the dancing that accompanied some of the festivals in the form of Morris men, who were reputedly the attendants of the King of the Wood. As the King, Jack in the Green, or the Green Man passed amongst the people, they were entertained by the Morris men who performed ritual dances and rhymes for their amusement. There is little doubt that many of these dances had roots in Pagan culture and were a distinctive part of the overall Green Man ethos. The origin of the word "morris" is obscure, but some sources have suggested that it may derive from the word "Moor" or "Blackamoor" (North African), especially because some dancers originally blackened their faces, perhaps to resemble Underworld spirits. In medieval times when Christianity was at war with Moorish Islam, this description would have held rather dubious connotations. Furthermore, many people of North African or Middle Eastern origin were believed to be skilled in the arts of Black Magic, herbs, and potions, and were greatly opposed to Christians. Therefore, the incorporation of such individuals into the revelries added a supernatural and dangerous note. The idea of the hostile Moor, concealed amongst the everyday medieval world (just as the Green Man himself was concealed amongst the foliage of the forest) must indeed have been a highly potent symbol, and may well have added weight to the image of concealment. But there were other, slightly dubious, associations too.

The Calusari

It has been argued that the origins of the Morris tradition began in Eastern Europe with a group or sect known as the *Calusari*.

This was—and by all accounts still is—an enigmatic group strongly connected with the forces of Nature. There is no exact translation for the name, but it is thought to mean "fairies" or "little horses," and refers to a kind of being that is part human and part of the Natural world. Described as "folk ritualists," the Calusari were apparently split into two principal groups. One branch seemed to embrace a form of Christianity, albeit tinged with a certain amount of Paganism. As anyone who had watched one particular episode of the popular series *The X-Files*, which bears the Calusari name, will know they chiefly concerned themselves with forms of exorcism and the driving out of evil spirits by ritual means. The other, older branch however, concerned itself with ritual dancing. This was reputedly a dance of the "animal men" and was said to follow certain Pagan traditions and styles. In some cases, and in remote areas of Romania, the Calusari dressed in animal skins and beat each other with wooden staves. They then processed through the various villages and districts where women brought out sick children for the beast-men to lay hands upon them and cure them. This action was widely believed to drive out the demons that caused the illness (especially in the very young), for the Calusari were thought to have healing powers and, similar to their later, more Christian contemporaries, the ability to exorcise evil.

Following the general healing sessions, the Calusari then performed further ritualized dances, which, according to some traditions, ended in a kind of symbolic wedding ceremony. In some instances, members of the Calusari troup, dressed in animal skins, forced their way into houses that they passed (this was usually done in a good-natured fashion), and refused to leave until they were fed with such things as fresh-baked bread and freshly drawn sweet milk.

Fresh vegetables might also be included, and in these offerings, the connection with the living, natural world providing for their wants and needs is obvious.

This practice was carried on by ritual groups who visited houses all over Europe and Britain on certain nights of the year. However, the Calusari were allegedly the only ones with healing and exorcism powers and were therefore treated reverentially. Many of the group were also supposed to have a specialized knowledge of both herbs and cures, and could be approached, at any time, in lieu of formal doctor, who were not available in rural areas or were far too expensive. The dance performed by these ritualists was believed to roughly correspond to that performed by Morris men in parts of England. All these connections—between countries as far apart as, say, England and Romania—exist as part of an overall Green Man idea and serve to demonstrate the Universality of the belief in the medieval and early modern world.

The Calusari may also have given us another concept. On May Eve and at May Day, in certain rural areas, some of the dancers placed a long pole between their legs and "galloped" about through various communities, grabbing young women and from time to time copulating with them. The phallic symbolism of the pole between the legs is obvious, and the practice seems to have given the Calusari their description of "little horses." This also gave rise to the celebrated Victorian children's toy—the hobbyhorse.

The Green Man and Legendary Figures

There were even further, questionable associations between the Green Man and certain historical and legendary figures. It has already been mentioned that Green Man festivals flourished in some parts of England following the restoration of King Charles II in 1660. The inferences here are obvious—the return of the king after a period of dour parliamentary rule, promising better times for all his subjects. There were other figures too who were portrayed as associates of the Green Man, especially during the May revelries.

King Arthur

King Arthur, the legendary 6th century monarch of Britain, took on a kind of Green Man persona and was feted in many revelries throughout rural England. There was an old legend that Arthur had never died but was "merely sleeping"—whether on the mystic Isle of Avalon or in several caves the length and breadth of England—and that he and his knights would rise once more in the country's time of need. In fact, there were some who believed that Arthur and his knights would rise during World War II when Hitler was poised across the English Channel, allegedly ready to invade. Around this time, there were a number of admittedly small "Arthurian Societies" formed to await such a return. The notion of a monarch, lying asleep in wait for a summons and then rising again when needed, of course, chimes in well with the notion of the King of the Wood and the victory of spring/summer over winter.

King Brute

Other monarchs too are sometimes associated with the Green Man. For instance, King Brute, a mythical ruler who allegedly drove the giants out of Britain and who defeated the Cornish giant Cormoran is another name that appears. Brute was allegedly

Brutus—alternately a survivor from either the sack of Carthage (in North Africa) or from the siege of Troy. Together with other surviving soldiers, he arrived in Britain following the withdrawal of the Roman legions, and seized power there, driving out localized "barbarian" kings. His last obstacles to total control of the country were the Cornish giants, led by their aging and grey-bearded king, the mighty Cormoran. Brute challenged Cormoran to a hand-to-hand battle on St. Michael's Mount, which lies on the southern tip of Cornwall. The battle lasted all day and all night, at last Cormoran was slain, falling from the Mount as a great thunderbolt and creating a tidal wave that partly cut it off from the mainland (it can now only be accessed by a causeway). However, Brute himself was gravely wounded in the fight and died soon afterward, according to some versions of the legend. In other variants, he returned victorious and ruled for a short time, afterward but was subsequently murdered by some of his followers who were jealous of him. He was buried in a secret location, where his decomposing body caused lush vegetation and beautiful flowers to grow. However, similar to Arthur, he may return if Britain requires him to stand in her defense. Again, the mythical linkage with the idea of the King of the Wood—the notion of death and resurrection at a critical time—is obvious.

King Vortigern

A similar story is told of King Vortigern, said to be the last British king before the coming of Arthur's father, Uthar Pendragon. (Other legends give this as Marcus Aurelius Ambrosius, or more properly Auerlianus Ambrosius, said to be a follower of the Manapiian, Carausius, an actual Anglo-Roman king 286–293.)

Similar to Brute, Vortigern also defeated giants and worked with magicians to transport the great pillars of Stonehenge from Ireland (where it was known as The Dance of the Giants) to Salisbury Plain in England. Vortigern, it is said, was a tyrant (the venerable Bede, writing in the 8th century, refers to him as "that proud tyrant") and leagued with the Saxons against Celtic Britain. Consequently, he was killed by his own people and his body buried in a lonely place. However, as a celebrated giant killer, Vortigern will return at some point if England is threatened once more.

The legends of Brute and Vortigern are again closely connected with the natural order of things, and it is small wonder that they should be associated with a Green Man-type figure. Even the name "Brute" is suggestive of a beast, and the fact that this king is supposed to have worn a wolf-skin compounds the image. Many of the stories concerning them date from the 12th and 13th centuries, chronicled by figures such as Geoffrey of Monmouth (c1100–c1155) or Ralph of Coggeshall (?–1227) who sought to connect Mankind with older and more supernatural traditions. However, both Geoffrey and Ralph, together with other chroniclers such as William of Newburgh (1136?–1198?), were simply using old tales they had heard in the countryside, and that were part of a Celtic tradition predated the monks by many centuries.

King Calgacos

In Scotland too, the legendary King Calgacos the Swordsman seems to have predated Arthur by many centuries. No dates are given for him, but he was defeated at Mon Gaupius (later misspelled as Mons Grampius, giving the Grampian Mountains their name) by the forces of the Roman military governor Julius Agricola in A.D. 84. Nothing is known of Calgacos except that his Celtic name was Clellach, and Roman historian Tacitus attributes a number of rather stirring speeches to him. Calgacos therefore is known as "the spirit of Scotland," and supposedly boasted a natural connection with Scottish soil. He is also described as "the swordsman" (not a widespread Celtic weapon) and supposedly carried a magic sword by which he could command Natural forces. Indeed, his court was supposedly held "in a wood," and although this may simply have been some sort of war camp, it may also have some sort of significance and connection to the Green Man.

Several Gaulish (early French) kings are also supposed to have connections with the earth and to be able to command Natural forces by virtue of their kingship. Some traditions say the same might be said of King Cassibelaunus, son of Heli and ruler of the Catuvellauni, a Celtic tribe living north of the River Thames. This notion is based on an account, written by Geoffrey of Monmouth, of an elaborate feast, which the king held in 53 B.C., in honor of his "victory" over the Roman forces of Julius Caesar. It is significant because it involved much ritual associated with nature and honored the Roman-Celtic sun god Belenus. Such feasts were supposed to convey great powers upon those who gave them.

King William II

Later, more historically based figures would also be vaguely equated with the Green Man. The English king, William II or William Rufus as he was known (1087–1100), the third son of William the Conqueror, for instance, was allegedly associated with ancient practices and was ritually put to death in the New Forest.

Interestingly, his "accidental" death (he was shot by the arrow of a companion, Walter Tyrell, while out hunting in the Forest) was similar to the ritual death of the King of the Wood. Therefore, the monarch was said to be the physical embodiment of the Green Man. This belief was given some credence when it was reported, as a hypothesis based on received tradition, by anthropologist Margaret Murray, author of the celebrated work *The Witch-cult in Western Europe* (1921), which generated much interest during the late 1960s and early 1970s, and which is still a significant text in the Neo-Pagan world. Based on Murray's hypothesis, many members of the English Royal Family had connections to the worship of the Horned God (which Christianity termed "the Devil"), who was a god of Nature. It was also believed that the death of William Rufus had been a ritualized sacrifice, carried out in the style of the King of the Wood, perhaps to ensure prosperity for the country and even that the Norman Conquest of England would succeed. This was, of course, simply speculation, but "deductions" surrounding William's rather mysterious death persist down to the present day. During the late 1960s, there were many attempts to link him to the ancient Pagan kings of Britain—all of them unsuccessful.

King Richard I

Other English monarchs have been touched by similar ancient speculations as well. Richard I ("Richard the Lionheart," 1189–1199) for example, has been spoken of in the same context as William II. Prior to departing on the Third Crusade in 1191, Richard is said to have done a private penance for an "unspeakable sin," which was said to be associated with the worship of other gods.

In actual fact, the penance may have been in respect to a homosexual act. (Scottish film star Sean Connery, who made a cameo
appearance as Richard in *Robin Hood, Prince of Thieves*, once wryly
remarked that this was the only time he had ever played an English
homosexual.) The idea of Richard and the embodiment of the Green
Man was so strong that some form of Pagan tradition was widely
suggested. Incidentally, homosexuality has been linked to the death
of William Rufus as well. The events surrounding Richard's death
in France were allegedly connected to ritual murder in the style of
the King of the Wood. This is not borne out by the historical facts.
Richard was killed while besieging the castle of Châlus Chabrol in
Limousin, and was grievously wounded by an arrow fired by one of
the stronghold's defenders, Pierre Basile. His death was simply a
military one and had no occult significance; yet all sorts of esoteric
speculation has attached to it.

Alexander Stewart

William and Richard were not the only monarchs or royal per-
sonages to have elements of sometimes dark Nature worship connected to their names. In Scotland, Alexander Stewart, the celebrated
Wolf of Badenoch, and brother to King Robert III (1390–1406),
supposedly consorted with Highland cailleachs (Witches and wise
women), and with demons and dark, Natural spirits in the great
stone circle at Kingussie in Speyside during the latter half of the
14th century. These may simply have been no more than tales put
about by Alexander Burr, Bishop of Moray, following the Wolf's
attack on the churches of Forres and Elgin, but they still remain
firmly in Speyside legend.

James III of Scotland

Similar stories abound regarding the enigmatic James III of Scotland (1460–1488). The manner of this complex monarch's mysterious death following the Battle of Sauchieburn has led to much speculation as to its actual circumstances—might it have anything to do with the sacrifice of the King of the Wood? Probably not. Although James is thought to have experimented with alchemy and Black Magic, along with having an interest in ancient mysteries, the times in which he lived were extremely turbulent and he had many enemies. Indeed, at Sauchieburn, he was fighting forces loyal to his own son—the future James IV. However, his character was such a complex one that it is not inconceivable that he might well have been involved in something akin to the Green Man ethos.

Nowadays, it is perhaps culturally acceptable to look on the Green Man as a sort of quaint, medieval image, a piece of ancient art or ornamentation that has little or no relevance to the present day. Nothing is further from the truth, for there is a Green Man deep in all of us. The image of the Green Man is an emblem of Mankind's fundamental split with the Natural world, and of attempts to reestablish that link. It is also emblematic of both a yearning and a fear that lies at the heart of human society—a wanting to be reunited with the Natural world and yet a fear of that very world. These dual aspects manifest themselves in art, tradition, and culture. Thus, foliage-shrouded heads, half-hidden figures, and ancient feasts and festivals become a strand of our culture. As do environmental issues, rising higher and higher on the current scales of political importance, and a longing look backwards to a simplified, less mechanized time. The Green Man in fact lies just under the surface of modern culture and at the very heart of our traditions and values. It is not a face from the past, but is actually an integral (if slightly concealed) part of our modern world.

Following in the theme of "quaintness," many people consider the Green Man a manifestation of the Celtic time or of "olde merrie England" and, while not altogether true, perhaps this serves as a useful starting point for our exploration of the figure.

Chapter 2

The Lurker Amongst the Leaves

For many people, the Green Man is an image strongly connected with one particular part of the world—England. Although it is also known as a symbol of the Celtic era and appears in other parts of the world, the Green Man, arguably more than any other image, is taken to represent "merrie England" and the boisterous medieval and early modern period. It is also seen as a largely rural image, representing perhaps the darker pastoral history of the country where extremely old ways and traditions are still observed.

This perception, though a relatively false one, is understandable. The image of the Green Man, as we have noted, has its roots in extremely ancient traditions, probably stretching as far back as the separation of Mankind from Nature. Britain itself is an ancient land, and part of its early history is swathed in mist and mystery. Ancient settlements, stretching back to the Bronze Age and beyond, are regularly unearthed in various parts of the English countryside, hinting at earlier mysteries, which archaeologists are still seeking to unravel. The dark and largely unknown 5th, 6th, and 7th centuries, the age when Arthur and his descendants are thought to have lived, continue to fascinate historians, mythologists, and folklorists alike, spawning all sorts of tales and speculations regarding the period. England, therefore, would appear to be fertile ground for the development of the Green Man idea.

As we have seen, the Green Man is a figure of the deep forest, and at one time much of England was covered in dark and gloomy woodland. Indeed, despite the advancement of technology, some of these ancient forests still exist, such as the New Forest, the Forest of Dean, and so forth. In former times, many of these forests and woodlands held tiny settlements, hamlets, and villages where people lived surrounded by trees. It was only natural, therefore, that tales of the woodland dark would form and crystallize in people's minds.

Although England is ostensibly a Saxon country, its origins lie in its dim and Celtic past. It shares a history with such areas as Wales, Scotland, Cornwall, Brittany and Ireland, where the Celtic traditions not only took root, but also where the Saxon influence was not as strong. However, in England the most ancient of all traditions contain Celtic elements.

The Trees and The Celts

For the Celts, spirits were everywhere in the Natural world. They were in springs, wells, rocks, and most potently in trees. There were few more important symbols in ancient lore than that of the tree. Amongst the Celts, the holy men were known as *Druids*, which in the Celtic tongue meant "men of the oak." These Pagan priests had a special affinity toward the oak trees, which for them was the symbol of wisdom and strength. In fact, some of these perceptions remain in our consciousness today—we speak of being "as strong as an oak tree" or of having "a heart of oak." In Ireland and in Scotland, people will still not cut down a lone tree to which they ascribe ancient powers (usually denoted as "the fairies," as in a "fairy thorn" or "skeagh," as it is known in some parts of Ireland and Scotland).

Possibly, some of the trees in the forests of ancient Britain took on strange forms. Many of us may have seen a tree, the trunk of which is extremely twisted, through either some damage or an eccentric growth, so that it's trunk resembles a human face. Coming upon such a growth in the dark depths of a forest may have been a terrifying experience, and may have led to a deep fear of or reverence for the place where the tree grew. It may indeed have become a site of awe and mystery for those early people. As well as the dark forests, there were groves of sacred trees where the Druids sometimes carried out their worship, scattered all over ancient England and the Celtic world. An old story from Glenflesk in North Kerry, Ireland, dating from around 1650, tells of how a group of Puritan troopers, part of the English Cromwellian army, rode into a certain grove of trees, surrounded by a large earthworks, which had been left undisturbed since the days of the Druids. It was twilight, and the troopers—all Englishmen—found themselves in the center of a grove of trees, the trunks of which all bore the faces of old men. In fact, it seemed as though these ancient growths were watching them closely, and though there was no wind several of them seemed to lean forward as if making closer inspection. The captain in charge, though quaking with fright, ordered his men to fire at the trees and to tumble the earthworks. This they did, and as the flames roared up, there came a series of unearthly shrieks from the trees around them. The entire troop was instructed to kneel and pray to God for deliverance from the horrible forces, which had been unleashed by the destruction. Such was the power of that ancient place and of the deformed trees.

Trees in Pagan and Christian Legend

Trees have always played an important part in ancient mythology and legend, both Pagan and Christian. In Norse mythology, for example, the World Tree, or Yggdrasil, connected the nine existences that straddled the worlds of gods and men with its mighty roots. Yggdrasil was reputedly a gigantic ash tree (and was the central feature of Norse cosmology), around the base of which the serpent Níôhöggr had twisted its body. The name Yggdrasil has been taken to mean "Odin's seed," and it was thought that the monstrous ash was the direct spawn of Odin, father of all the Norse gods. In Baltic folklore too, we find examples of mystical trees. Latvian tales tell of the Austras Koks (tree of the east or tree of the dawn), a mystical tree that flourished only while the sun was in the sky. It grew as soon as the sun rose and withered and died as it set, ready to spring into life the following day. It was said to grow away in the east of the country on the banks of the Daugava River.

In Semitic folklore too, the tree loomed large, and here it was considered to be a symbol of age and wisdom. It is no coincidence that the center of the Garden of Eden is the Tree of the Knowledge of Good and Evil from which Adam and Eve eat in Genesis. It is from this tree that they gain knowledge of the wider cosmos, and of their place within it. They also gain an understanding of their own unsophistication. Again, as in Norse and other mythologies, the serpent plays a large part. It is the Shaitan (the Enemy) that lurks amongst the leaves of the Tree of the Knowledge of Good and Evil to bring death and destruction to both Adam and Eve by tempting Eve with its honeyed words. It is the symbol of both power and death, for in eating the fruits of Knowledge, both Adam and Eve lose their immortality. There is a potent symbolism here, which was common in the folklore of many ancient peoples. By enticing them to eat the fruit of the Tree of Knowledge, the serpent confers both their full potential as individuals, also their own mortality and decay. Just as Níôhöggr seeks to destroy the central core of the world by devouring the roots of Yggdrasil, so the Shaitan seeks to destroy the epitome of God's creation.

Throughout the Celtic world, however, trees (particularly misshapen trees) cast a long shadow in both folklore and poetry. In many of the ancient poetic writings of Ireland, for instance, no less than five sacred trees are named. These growths appear to have been known through the length and breadth of the country in both folklore and literature. They were the Tree of Ross, the Tree of Mugna, the Tree of Dathi, the Tree of Usnach, and the Tree of Tortu. There were undoubtedly other, lesser growths scattered throughout the countryside. In folklore, the Tree of Ross (a massive ash-tree—similar to Yggdrasil, which was also said to be an ash) was extremely revered by the Druids and had oracular properties, granting visions of the future to those who slept under its branches. In another account, the mighty Oak of Mugna was "overturned by the poets and bards," presumably to prevent it from being cut down as a Pagan image by the axes of Christian monks. It was from the Oak that many of the bards and rhymers apparently drew their inspiration.

The other mighty trees were either destroyed by the incoming Christians, who probably saw them as a focus for Pagan worship, or by their own followers to prevent them from falling into Christian hands. The great Ash of Usnach was said to have been destroyed during the reign of the sons of Aed Slane (probably late 5th or early 6th centuries). Others may have been destroyed even earlier. And apart from Ireland, there are legends of other trees in Scotland, Brittany, and in areas of Wales, which fulfilled the same votive functions, and which were similarly destroyed. Thus, trees were an important and centralizing force in the Celtic world, often confirming a sense of identity and cohesion for those who worshipped them, prior to the coming of Christianity. Moreover, the tree became connected to worship and offering, and the gods became inextricably linked with the deep, dark, forest and with growth. Legend tells us that in early Germany, St. Wilibrod was so appalled at the worship of and human sacrifice (usually of children) of trees, that he instructed the Christ Child to be placed on the top of certain trees and for all human sacrifice to stop. However, he still allowed gifts to be laid there. Therein, is it said, lie the Christian origins of the festive Christmas tree.

Beings in the Trees

Fertility, wonder, and awe had become linked with the tree and with the deep forest. At the height of the summer, when things were growing, many trees boasted lush and verdant foliage, the symbol of vigorous life. Of course, this provided a cover in which all kinds of supernatural beings connected with the tree might be hiding. These were usually taken, using the imagery of ancient Rome, to be dryads, or personifications of the life force of the tree itself. They moved almost invisibly along the branches and trunk of the tree, well-protected and hidden by the leafy growth all around. They dropped fruit and nuts on any human who might be resting, sleeping, or sheltering under the encompassing boughs, but when sought out with the eye, they darted away to be lost in the gloom of the foliage. Many of them were harmless, simply mischievous, but they were the protectors of the tree and might take vengeance on anyone who harmed it or sought to cut it down. Some of them could, therefore, be incredibly malicious and hostile toward humans whom they viewed as destroying the forests, and consequently their Natural habitat. This chimed in well with general perception, with the malevolent gods of the woodland deeps. Things scurried and scampered amongst the leafy branches, heard but usually unseen by travelers through the forests. The furtive movements of hidden creatures became the movements of strange and elemental beings who, like it or not, intended humans some harm.

In his genuinely chilling story *The Ash Tree*, the classic ghost story writer M.R. James hints at strange creatures who live among, the branches of an ancient tree and who seek to invade a house—the suggested "guests at the Hall." The tree itself positively exudes an air of menace and threat. For such an eerie effect, James may well have been drawing upon that centuries-old tradition and belief regarding strange creatures living in the trunks or amongst the branches of certain trees. Their presence, it seems, was widely felt and was usually threatening. These creatures, sheltering in the gloom, provided a fitting basis for the idea of the Green Man.

The Wild Hunt

The Huntsman and the Herdsman

There was another strand to this belief too. As Man began to move away from the Nature of which he had once been a part, he began to assume a kind of "mastery" over it—particularly over the animals with which he had once competed for food. Indeed, the Christian Bible explicitly gives him "lordship" over "the beasts of the field." The man who could claim mastery over animals was indeed powerful. The idea may have arisen out of certain Shamanistic notions, in which the Shaman or Witch doctor could provide, by supernatural means, a productive hunt through calling animals from the forest to be captured. Later, the idea assumed a wider "mastery."

Two people who could control animals stood out. One of these was the huntsman—the man who, by his skill and cunning, tracked down animals and slew them, thus providing food for his community. The hunter also represented wildness—the wildness of the chase across the plain or through the forest in the unbridled pursuit of prey. Not surprisingly, the idea of the hunt and of the huntsman found its way into folklore. Thus we see in places such as Germany and England the idea of the Wild Hunt, led either by the Devil or some other supernatural figure. This reckless chase hunted down human souls across the skies and all were advised to stay indoors until the Hunt had passed, lest they be taken with it and never seen again. In this, the Wild Hunt and similar chases represented the wildness of Nature, free and unfettered, travelling with the wind (in a number of places it was equated with the wind) between the trees of the forest or across the open plains. The frequency of the belief in the Wild Hunt only serves to underline the strength of this perception.

The second "wild figure" that appears in folklore with a control over animals is that of the herdsman. Similar to the huntsman, the herdsman had a "mastery" over the animals in his charge and indeed, he might well have been considered more powerful because he could guide them and often get them to do his bidding. In other words, he could command them, just as God (and certain other supernatural beings) had intended. The herdsman was in fact a very potent symbol of control and power. It is no coincidence that Jesus is often referred to as "the Good Shepherd"—a symbol of the ultimate herdsman. However, once again, the herdsman also represented the "wildness" of Nature. Many herdsmen and shepherds lived with their flocks and herds out in the open. In the wilderness, where their animals grazed, they were often isolated from civilization, and in many cases remained so close to the animals they protected that they may have been thought to have taken on some of the attributes of such creatures. They were also fiercely protective of the creatures they looked after, driving away predators and scavengers with an almost feral attitude. In this, they almost seemed to represent "the spirit of the wild," a basis for the Green Man.

Herne, the Wild Huntsman

The idea of the hunter, the herdsman, and the trees sometimes coalesced. One of those figures who led the Wild Hunt was an entity known as Herne. He was the Wild Huntsman, leading a crowd of followers across the skies (he had taken over the role, to some extent, from Oden, father of the Norse gods, who led a similar hunt) and was sometimes known as the Green Huntsman. Although probably a very early mythological figure, the first mention of Herne occurs in Shakespeare's *Merry Wives of Windsor*. In Act 4, Scene IV,

Herne

Mistress Page recounts the following legend:

> *There is an old tale goes that Herne the Hunter,*
>
> *Sometime a keeper here in Windsor forest,*
>
> *Doth all the winter-time, at still midnight,*
>
> *Walk round about an oak, with great ragg'd horns;*
>
> *And there he blasts the tree and takes the cattle,*
>
> *And makes milch-kine yield blood and shakes a chain*
>
> *In a most hideous and dreadful manner:*
>
> *You have heard of such a spirit, and well you know*
>
> *The superstitious idle-headed eld*
>
> *Received and did deliver to our age*
>
> *This tale of Herne the hunter for a truth.*

Akin to many of his generation, Shakespeare was fascinated by folklore, and as such plays as *MacBeth* and *Hamlet* show, he had a particular interest in matters relating to ghosts, spirits, and the supernatural. And he did not waste any time incorporating these into his work. The tale of Herne the Hunter was probably well-known in Shakespeare's time. The fact that he wears "ragg'd horns" is suggestive of a much earlier, prehistoric time when a Shaman may have dressed himself in animal skins and antlers to mimic a creature that he and his clan worshipped. By doing this and by adding some form of ritual to it, he supernaturally ensured good hunting for his fellow clan members. In the previous extract, Herne appears to be some form of ghost identified with a former keeper in the Windsor area—perhaps in charge of the deer or other animals that grazed there. However, the addition of the horns or antlers is significant for a number of reasons. First, they identified Herne with the animal kingdom, particularly the stag whose potency and vigor many ancient peoples admired. Stags were usually venerated in spring when the rutting took place, and when they were often at their most aggressive. Indeed, the stag became almost symbolic of the two aspects of sex and strength. Second, the horn is a very ancient symbol, representing the male penis and as such is a symbol of virility and procreation. To wear them was a confirmation of lustiness and vitality. Thirdly, the wearing of the horns amongst hunters was also seen as a mark or reward for slaying the greatest number of animals. Here, hunters took the skin of their prey and any other part that could be removed and worn, in the hope that some of the beast's prowess would in some way transfer itself to them.

Thus, given all this extremely loaded symbolism, Shakespeare's Herne becomes something more than the simple ghost of some former forestry warden; he becomes the embodiment of all the ancient and potent natural forces. He becomes in effect, a form of the Green Man.

Herne, the stag-man, indeed had a pedigree, which stretched much further back than Shakespeare's time. In the 1400s, there were many stories of the Wild Hunt and of its leader, the Horned Man whom Christians later categorized as the Devil. In fact, the notion of horns (or antlers) was to become synonymous with evil and malignancy in Christian mythology. The Horned Man—probably a folk memory of the ancient antlered Shamans—quickly became Herne the Hunter, who presided over the wild company who rushed relentlessly through the storm-tossed skies of the winter months.

In Shakespeare's play, he is also associated with a certain tree in Windsor Forest (now Windsor Great Park). This is another folkloric belief—that Herne was connected in some way to certain trees, which were then worshipped in his name. Indeed, the tree at Windsor was well-known as "Herne's Oak," certainly until the 17th (or even 18th) century, and there were a number of other similarly named trees scattered across the English countryside. It was said that the Wild Hunt visited these trees and used them as rallying points in their chase. In a sense, Herne and his pack represented the wildness of nature—the unbridled force that permeated all living and growing things.

The idea of the wild leader and his followers easily translated into other cultures and into other forms. In Sweden, he became a wild tree-like creature at the head of a pack of baying dogs who continually hunted through the forests; in Russia, he became a grim huntsman whose stone heart lay in a casket in the center of an island in the middle of an underground lake. In Wales too, he became Arawn, King of the Underworld and Lord of the Dead, who continually rode out from his dread domain with a pack of hounds. Arawn was encountered by the celebrated Pwyll, Prince of Dyffd, and their meeting is recounted in a poem of the same name. The Huntsman is also another name for Gwynn ap Nudd, who is said to dwell beneath Glastonbury Tor, leading either a group of other hunters or a pack of hounds to hunt in the more cultivated lands around the Tor on certain days of the year—usually ancient feast days. Legends say that, on each visit, he took a beautiful girl back with him to his lightless kingdom.

In some cases, the Huntsman was identified with figures of the dead—a deceased warrior or ancient berserker—vaguely remembered by certain communities. In medieval times, the spirit of Harald Halt-foot, an ancient Norse warrior, terrorized the east of England, with a host of Undead companions. Their hunt was a kid of "ramscutter"—a wild and uproarious chase, during which they plundered and robbed various houses along the way. Sometimes Harald was portrayed with horns or antlers that grew from his forehead; at other times wearing a great horned helmet, the symbol of a fierce and aggressive Nature. And Herne appears in other guises as well— often he is riding a wild horse and is followed by a pack of wolves or a group of wild men. Sometimes, his followers wore green cloaks and hoods to conceal themselves as they rushed through the woodlands. Beings such as Herne are therefore widely regarded as the God of the Hunt, and as a representation of the Natural world, or indeed, a God of the Forest.

It was not a great step from the Wild Huntsman to the Green Man. Lurking amongst the woodlands, waiting to trap his prey, Herne became little more than a face amongst the leaves—a symbol of the prehistoric hunter continually waiting and watching. Although the huntsman and the herdsman were, as the embodiment of wildness, very old figures, there were other ancient elements that also made up this impression.

The Wild Man in Ancient Times

Wildness and Wild Men have a long tradition stretching back into Babylonian times. The character of Enkidu appears in the ancient Sumerian *Epic of Gilgamesh* (written around 700 B.C.) as a primitive, almost unbiddable figure, a companion to Gilgamesh, the hero-king of the saga. Rough and uncouth, is nonetheless possessed a formidable and almost supernatural strength, as well as animal-like skill and cunning that made him almost something of a trickster. After killing the sacred Bull of Heaven, he is killed in vengeance by the gods, and his death prompts Gilgamesh to enter the Otherworld in order to find a cure for age and death. This cure comes in the form of a plant known only as "The Old Man Has Become Young Again," which only grows in the supernatural realm. Although Gilgamesh finds the plant, he loses it to a serpent that tricks him. Many of the Natural elements, which appear in Christian mythology, are also to be found here. In many respects, Enkidu might be considered as one of the earliest forms of the Green Man.

Osiris

Certain elements of Sumerian tradition would influence the later Egyptian civilization. The color green had strong connotations in Egyptian folklore. It was a color that was associated with doing the positive or correct thing. It was also associated with vegetation, the Natural order, and with resurrection. It was the color of Osiris, possibly the most important of all the Egyptian deities, who was killed by his brother Set, but who rose again, defeating Death. (Set was also one of the principal gods of the Hyksos—a series of Middle Eastern overlords who ruled Egypt for a time.) Osiris's resurrection was connected, it was said, with the flood cycle of the Nile Delta, when the river rose and flooded the plains. Afterward, there was new growth and lush vegetation—a symbol of Osiris's connection with rebirth and with growing things. The connection with the Green Man is obvious.

It is also worth noting that the green Osiris "became" his son Horus—the progeny of his marriage to the goddess Isis. In some folklore, Osiris was slain and cut to pieces shortly after to be fully reborn as Horus, thus completing the circle of death and rebirth. In his Horus incarnation, the god retains elements of his mother Isis, thus becoming both masculine and feminine—both the Green Man and the Green Woman. Osiris would go on to become the Lord of the Underworld in Egyptian mythology, in charge of the souls of the dead in the afterlife.

This complicated folk belief first appeared in the 4th Pharaohic Dynasty (roughly from around 2575–2467 B.C.), but it is possible that Osiris was older than that. Indeed, it is possible that the name came from that of an actual monarch who ruled the Nile Delta in a prehistoric time. The original god may well have been known as Andjety, who was an early fertility deity embodying untamed and wild Nature. Both Andjety and Osiris may have been an Egyptian version of the Green Man, which passed down into later folklore in the West.

Dionysus

Greek mythology too had elements of wildness enshrined in it. The Nature god Dionysus dwelt in the wild and had certain animalistic elements about him, including having the cloven feet of a goat or sheep (that is, cloven-hoofed). There were certain legends that said the god ate human flesh, especially the flesh of young infants. In one tale, for instance, the three daughters of King Minyas were reluctant to honor Dionysus or to obey his call for human sacrifice, and furthermore scolded other women for doing so. For this impiety the god extracted a terrible revenge upon them. He first confronted them as a raging bull, then as a lion, and lastly as a swift and ferocious leopard. He then covered the seats on which they sat with vines and ivy, and filled the baskets in which they kept their wool with snakes, scorpions, and other woodland creatures. The terrified women offered up one of their children to Dionysus, and after drawing one, he tore the unfortunate child to pieces. Their deed earned them the revulsion of their people and they were cast out into the wild. There they were metamorphosized by Dionysus himself into a bat, an owl, and a crow—once again, images of the wild and of the forest. In fact, the legend may relate to a number of Nature-worship cults (amalgamated under the name of "Dionysus," which may have practiced human or child sacrifice and were later outlawed under Greek law). Later, Dionysus would be transformed into the goat-footed Roman god Pan or Bacchus—the god of wine and of licentious (unbridled) behavior.

Buile Shuibhne

Celtic mythology too, held stories concerning figures that "became wild" and ran off to live in the wilderness as a "wild man." The most famous of these was a king—Buile Shuibhne. Shuibhne, a son of the Irish monarch Colman Cuar, was king of Dal Araidhe, a kingdom in the North of Ireland. According to legend, he took a great dislike to Ronan the Cleric, an early Christian holy man who dwelt at the church of Cill Luinne, and Shuibhne attacked the church and the cleric's house. Worse, in a fit of anger, he took Ronan's beautifully illustrated missal and threw it into a large cold-water lake (traditionally stated to be Lough Neagh) or into a well where it was lost. This was an act of great blasphemy and the cleric had no other choice but to curse the king, taking away his senses. Shuibhne now believed himself to be a bird and took to living in trees and dwelling in the wilderness—becoming, in effect, a "wild man." The tale dates from around the time of the Battle of Moira (A.D. 637) between the Ui Niall and the forces of the Scottish king Dumnhaill Brec. However, it was not written down until some time between 1200 and 1500, possibly by monks or scribes intent on recording old and important legends. A translation of the story also forms the basis for *Sweeney Astray*, a work by the Northern Irish poet Seamus Heaney. The idea of a mad king living out in the wild amongst the forests and bogs fits in well with the idea of the Green Man and indeed the notion of the King of Nature—an enemy of Christianity in the medieval period when the story was being written down—and may have served as the original motif.

Medieval Men

Merlin

A similar legend exists concerning another more celebrated Celtic mythological figure—Merlin, the Wizard at the Court of King Arthur. Despite being renowned as a venerable sage and a wise counselor, Merlin (or Myrdinn in ancient Celtic) has a much more checkered history. His origins are shrouded in mystery, but it is quite possible that he was Welsh, having crossed the border into Celtic Britain. Part of this belief may be attributed to Geoffrey of Monmouth, who gives the first fully developed account of his life in his *Libellus Merline* (*Little Book of Merlin*) written around 1135. This also formed the basis for Geoffrey's allegorical Latin poem *Vita Merlini*

(Life of Merlin), which was written in 1150 and is an extremely complex prophetic text written, arguably, in the style of the Welsh bards. Based on the *Vita*, Geraldus Cambrensis (Gerald of Wales), penning a work on the Merlin figure around 1185, confidently asserts that there were in effect two Merlins—one being the austere sage and the other being a wild man who lived in the wilderness.

Arthur was not the only early British king to whom Merlin was tutor or advisor. It has been suggested that he was tutor—perhaps in a military sense—to King Vortigern and also to King Gwenddoleu, an ancient king of Britain who may have had Druidic connections. This ruler fought against two of his cousins, Gwrgi and Peredur, at the Battle of Arfderydd in A.D. 575 (the name is taken to mean "lark's nest," possibly the site of the Scottish medieval port of Caerlaverlock—about 9 miles south of Dumfries), during which he was killed. Also slain in the course of the conflict were Merlin's two brothers who led two of the Six Faithful Companies of Britain and, driven wild with grief, he forsook the royal court and fled into the wild. In some versions of the tale he was accompanied by his sister Gwenddydd, who looked after him during his time of madness.

The Faithful Companies continued to fight on in Gwenddoleu's name for another six weeks until they were finally defeated by superior numbers, but Merlin took no part in this conflict, preferring to live in the deepest woods, subsisting on berries and grass. During this time, he is supposed to have communicated with forest spirits and learned many natural secrets, which would be of great value to him later in life at Arthur's court. He was also reputedly known as Merlin Wylt or Merlin Wold (Merlin the Wild) during this period. Later, the madness would pass and he would return to civilization and settle down, but the insights he had gained from living in the forest, together with the knowledge he had obtained from the forest deities, would never leave him and would turn him into the great sage, the guise by which he is most widely known. The face of the Wild Man, imbued with the knowledge that both Nature and madness brings, is reminiscent of the face of the Green Man, peering out from amid the leaves of the forest.

The Wild Men of the Forest

The Wodewose

During the early medieval period, it is quite possible that there were groups of people—or "Wildmen"—who lived in the depths of the forests, which covered a large part of England. These were perhaps people who found life in the towns intolerable, and who enjoyed the freedom of the forests and swamps. Those who lived in the towns and cities unquestionably viewed these people with a mixture of suspicion and alarm. These were the "wild folk" who lived beyond the pale of civilization and were only marginally removed from animals. One grouping in particular engendered terror amongst townspeople and travelers alike. They were the "wodewose," gangs of armed men who lived deep in the woodlands and made their living by robbing those who journeyed between the towns along the twisting forest paths that led through their domain. According to tradition it was not only travelers who were in danger, for the wodewose allegedly attacked churches and monastic houses, believing them to contain wealth, and they earned themselves the approbation of the Church. As it did with every other enemy or those whom it disliked, the Church began to circulate rumors about these

wild men—that they ate small children or that they worshipped the
Devil or forest gods deep in the heart of the woodlands. In fact,
according to some accounts, some of the wodewose wore green cloaks
and green hoods in order to disguise themselves in the forest and
avoid detection and capture. This became connected in the eyes of
the Church with the followers of the Wild Hunt or with those who
worshipped the strange, Pagan forest gods, placing the wodewose
well outside the bounds of Christianity.

Robin Hood

These "wild men of the forest" would eventually become embodied in a single figure that has survived down the years to the
present day—Robin Hood, the outlaw of Sherwood Forest. It should
be pointed out that although no real historical evidence exists for
such a figure (in fact, Robin Hood may well be an amalgam of medieval heroic figures), he has become something of a national figure, giving his name to a bay and even an English airport. Across
the centuries, much has been added to the Robin Hood legend—
that he was a swashbuckling hero in the style of Errol Flynn; that he
fought the tyrannical King John who was ruling England during
the absence of his brother Richard I; that he was the Earl of Loxley
who fought the corrupt Sheriff of Nottingham, and therefore
became a national hero. Such legends have persisted down to the
present day, even forming the basis of Kevin Costner's 1991 epic
Robin Hood: Prince of Thieves. However, it is extremely doubtful
that any of these legends are true. Robin Hood belongs to a series of
medieval outlaw-hero tales, stretching all the way back into Saxon
times and including such luminaries as Hereward the Wake, Fulk
FitzWarin, and Eustace the Monk (who may have served as a prototype

for Friar Tuck in the Robin Hood tales). Arguably, the basis of the Robin Hood legend is to be found in a ballad or long poem known as *The Tale of Gamelyn* written by an unknown poet around about the 14th century and concerning another fabled outlaw. Unlike the stories that preceded him, such as Fulk FitzWarin (who was a renegade baron) or Eustace the Monk (who was an abbot), Gamelyn is a wandering knight who joins the wodewose, eventually becoming their leader. Many of his exploits parallel those of Robin Hood, and are tales of high adventure rather than magical and mystical stories (as are those concerning Eustace). Indeed, the bare bones of the *Gamelyn* story may have formed the basis for the later *The Ballads of Robin Hood*, which date from around the 15th and 16th centuries.

The name itself is suggestive—"Robin Hood" may have originally been cited as "Robin in a hood," a reference to the hoods worn by the followers of the Nature gods or of those following the Wild Hunt. It was perhaps used by the Church to denote the Paganism of some of those who dwelt in the forest depths. Of course, as has been frequently pointed out, the name Hud or Hudd may have been a proper name—as in the roots of the surname Hudson (Hudd's son), which was later corrupted into the more genteel Hood. So the legendary Robin Hood may be little more than the more commonplace Robert Hudd. Indeed, Hudd is still a surname in England, as in the British comedian Roy Hudd. Nevertheless, the name itself became imbued with a special significance, as did the color of his garb—Lincoln green—linking him inextricably to the Green Man and Pagan times.

One of the earliest known appearances of Robin Hood himself appears in the long poem *Piers Plowman* in 1377, attributed to

William Langland. The poem is written in "passus" (Latin for "steps" or long segments), and is counted as one of the earliest allegorical poems, even predating Geoffrey Chaucer. In this, Sloth, the lazy priest, notes that he knows "right well" tales and rhymes of Robyn Hud (sic), and so tales of the character must have been reasonably well-known by that time. The next reference to him is to be found in the *Wyntoun Scottish Chronicle* (written around 1420). This account links him to Lytle John and states that they dwell in "Yngl wode or Barrysdale" in the North of England, close to the Scottish border. This has led many Scots to claim that some of the tales of Robin Hood actually refer to the Scottish hero William Wallace. Although not necessarily associated with Sherwood Forest near Nottingham until much later, Robin Hood is certainly a figure of the deep woodlands and was probably associated, in some minds at least, with the ancient forest gods.

The main description of his life comes from a long ballad known as the *Lyttel Gest* (or *Geste*) *of Robin Hood* (roughly translating to "A life of Robin Hood"), which first appeared in printed form somewhere around 1492. It is part of a series of such songs and poems, collectively known as *The Ballads of Robin Hood,* which date from around that time. By then, Robin Hood had become something of a folk figure—sometimes a trickster or a person who went about in disguise to hoodwink the authorities, but essentially a good man who protected his people from tyranny. But he was always a figure of the forest, strongly associated with trees and woodlands. He was supposedly a shadow in the glades and along the gloomy forest growth, and as such was a fitting medieval successor to the Green Man. Indeed, he was to become known as the Lord of the Wildwood, a name that held definite overtones of the King of the Wood.

Much of this heroic figure or "gentleman outlaw" image owes much to the *Lyttel Gest*. Within the poem, Robin lays down (with kingly authority) a code of conduct that his Merry Men—or followers—must follow. In this he becomes a figure almost similar to King Arthur and his Knights of the Round Table. Part of the instruction is to always do right and help those who are in need—this is probably a much later addition in order to make Robin a hero who would appeal to Christians and perhaps take away some of his Pagan associations. However, the ancient undertones of Paganism still lingered for Robin's first target, Sir Richard-at-Lee, a greedy and corrupt churchman, the abbot of St. Mary's Abbey in York. Later, a Christian holy man in the guise of Friar Tuck was added to the band of Merry Men to give the legend and the concomitant ballads some form of Christian significance. The name "Tuck" may be derived from another outlaw or "wodewose" (man of the forest), Richard Stafford, who sometimes went under the name of Frere Tuk" (also rendered as Tulke). Indeed, some of the tales concerning Tuck in Robin's band may be more accurately attributed to Stafford, whom it is thought may have been a disgraced cleric. The point at which Friar Tuck actually joins the Merry Men (Robin's band of wodewose) is given in the poem/play fragment *The Ballads of Robin Hood and the Curtal Friar of Fountains Abbey* that supposedly dates from around 1475. It ends with the friar disappearing off to Greenwood to join Robin's band as a kind of confessor. The inclusion of Friar Tuck within the Merry Men is arguably an attempt to "Christianize" the Robin Hood legends and to give them a more acceptable aspect to the medieval mind. Thus, the tales were preserved within a religious ethos and not simply as Pagan stories.

The addition of Little John to the overall legend is an interesting one too. At one time it was thought that Little John might be Scottish—hence the folkloric connections with such folk heroes as William Wallace or Murray the Outlaw, who reputedly roamed the border country. However, in most of the tales he is portrayed largely as a giant of a man and rather wild and uncouth in his ways. He is, in many respects, the "wild man" of the forest—the true wodewose, a personal juxtaposition to the now more "sophisticated" or more "civilized" Robin Hood. He becomes a companion to Robin, even a second-in-command, but still retains something of the wildness of the forest about him. Possessed of a phenomenal strength (he defeats Robin in a battle of quarterstaves at a river crossing), woodland knowledge, and guile, although no real military strategist (that was the province of Robin alone), he was the Enkidu to Robin's Gilgamish. But it was through the figure of Little John that the spirits of untamed Nature remain, as the exploits of his leader become more and more representative of "civilized society" and "courtly conduct." It is interesting to note that in some of the ballads, it is Little John who urges attacks on churchmen and church properties—maybe an attempt to reassert certain Pagan values once more over those of the admittedly greedy Church officers.

Although recounting in detail many of Robin Hood's exploits, the *Lyttel Gest* deals with his death, at the hands of the Prioress (or Abbess) of Kirklees Abbey, only briefly. However, another ancient ballad—*The Ballad of the Death of Robyn Hoode*—deals with it a little more fully. Even here, the story is rather confusing and is often contradictory, suggesting later omissions and additions.

Roughly speaking, one version of the story is as follows: Growing old, suffering from many wounds and sensing that death might be near, Robin journeys to see a "kinswoman," who is the Prioress of Kirklees Abbey near Peterborough, and who is famed throughout the countryside as a noted healer. Little John, suspicious of the Prioress and her motives, urges Robin not to go, or if he does, to take a group of armed men with him as escort. Robin ignores this advice and arrives at Kirklees Abbey with only Little John as his companion.

On the way to the Abbey, they encounter a strange old woman washing clothes at a river crossing. She issues a curse upon them as they ride by her, which terrifies Little John. The hag is suggestive of the ancient Celtic goddess Clotha (from whom the River Clyde in Scotland takes its name), who was supposed to foretell the death of great heroes and who probably served as a prototype for the Irish banshee. Although Little John pleads with Robin to go back, his leader will not do so. They arrive at Kirklees where Robin is taken into a room to be healed while Little John has to wait outside. The Prioress begins to bleed her patient—the letting of blood was a common means of curing in medieval England. However, she deliberately bleeds him too much—Robin is an old man and is very weak. Little John eventually breaks in but finds his master in a dangerously weakened state and close to death. Realizing that the Prioress has betrayed them, perhaps for money, he pleads with Robin to allow him to burn Kirklees and kill her, but his leader refuses—he has never made war on a woman and will not do so now. However, he is still bleeding badly and his blood is seeping into the ground, so he asks Little John to take him to a window and to bring him his longbow. From the window of the Abbey, he shoots an arrow and declares that wherever it falls will be his grave. Little John carries out this duty, marking the grave with a large standing stone in the manner of ancient Celtic kings.

In this version of his end, Robin Hood dies by bleeding to death—a ritual method of human sacrifice in the Pagan world. Indeed, throughout the ancient world (and into modern times) the spilling of blood became strongly associated with sacrifice. Once again, this image fits in well with the ritual slaying of the King of the Wood, the blood spilling into the ground ensuring that there would be a good harvest the next year. And although the woman involved in his death is portrayed as a Christian Prioress, she may just as well be a Pagan priestess who may have overseen the ritual killing of the King.

Later versions of the story, perhaps dating from the 16th and 17th centuries, seem to have "sanitized" the original tale, yet still contain significant folkloric elements. A weak Robin, dying of old age and infirmity, lies under his favorite Greenwood tree, a great oak tree, and once again calls for his longbow. Propping his back against the tree, he uses the leverage to shoot an arrow off and where it lands, there he is buried, as in the previous story. This story connects Robin with the trees of the forest, particularly with the mighty oak. In some variants of the tale, Little John buries Robin standing up as in the fashion of a Celtic chieftain.

The old woman whom Robin and Little John encounter at the river crossing is once again a figure of early Celtic folklore. As had already been noted, she may represent an ancient Celtic death goddess who was probably the prototype of the banshee. It is said that such creatures only appeared to and interacted with those who were of regal descent or who had kingly or noble blood in their veins. Because she appears to issue a curse against Robin, this effectively places him within the context of an ancient Celtic monarch or noble—perhaps an acknowledgement of his perception as the King of the Wood.

In tradition, then, the figure of Robin Hood becomes inextricably entwined with the forest and with Natural things. He dwells in the Greenwood, he is a huntsman of deer, and he has a respect for living things. In actual fact, he might be counted as the very embodiment of Nature, in the same manner as Herne, Master of the Wild Hunt. Indeed, the similarity between the two was strengthened when Robin was accompanied by a band of Merry Men, also huntsmen, who were reminiscent of the Wild Hunt. Initially, he may well have been seen as an embodiment of the Natural forces, but as time went on and the figure of legend became more "sophisticated," that mantle may have passed to his bosom companion Little John. In fact, at the end of life, it is Little John who lays him to rest in the Greenwood, thus returning him to the Natural world. In this respect, then, Robin Hood may be seen as the representation of the Natural world and its protector. In fact, he may be seen as a later form of the Green Man, which has continued down in various forms across the years to the present day. Perhaps it is *his* head (or that of his successor Little John) that peers out from amongst the forest foliage as the Natural spirit of the woodland.

Nature's "Defenders"

While Robin Hood was certainly a more humanized expression of the Green Man during medieval times, he was not the only one. Nor was he the only protector of Nature in the medieval mind. There may well have been a number of other figures who dwelt deep within the forests. These were, as we have mentioned, the images of ancient forest gods—Nacht Ruprecht or Black Peter—odd, half-human, almost nebulous beings. This was well in keeping with the old disembodied forces in which many ancient peoples believed. As the medieval period wore on, however, such figures began to take on a more concrete and definite form, especially in England. Such a form was usually human—one that everyone knew and understood. We have already mentioned the wodewose, the "wild men" of the forest, but some forces took the form of giants or of mysterious knights and warriors. These, in turn, became "defenders" of Nature in a physical or military sense—standing against those who sought to desecrate or destroy it. They might also "test" men to see if they were worthy to share the world with Natural forces, and as such, might well be considered to be representations of old gods, assessing the worthiness of their followers. Similar to Robin Hood, some of these would also make their way into the literature of the time.

Sir Gawain and the Green Knight

Sometime during the 14th century, a lengthy poem concerning one of these "champions" appeared in England. Its plot might be rather flippantly described as a "test and quest" fable, and it reflected the harsher, darker side of the Green Man. The basis for the fable is rooted in Celtic mythology and legend, and concerns the court of King Arthur, who was said to be one of the last Celtic kings of Britain. It is entitled *Sir Gawain and the Green Knight*, although some folklorists have argued that the word "knight" is a much later addition, and that the work was originally entitled *Sir Gawain and the Green Gome* (the word "gome" being a medieval one, no longer in use, meaning "man"). It is a fable containing such a beauty of prose and strength of imagery that it has survived into modern times and is still required reading for all those who would seriously study Arthurian mythology. Indeed, it appears in several university courses as a part of Medieval and English Studies.

Sir Gawain

Although it is not altogether clear who wrote this text, it is believed to have been written somewhere in the area of Cumbria in the north of England and may date from around the mid-1300s. Significantly, this is also a period when many of the best foliate heads that appeared in churches and monasteries were thought to have been carved, and may therefore indicate an increased level of interest in the Green Man. Again, the story reflects the changing seasons and the distinction between the green of summer and the bleakness of winter.

The adventure begins as Arthur and his knights sit down to a grand banquet around Christmastime in Camelot. As they begin to eat, a terrifying figure rides into their hall with a sound like the crash of thunder. This is a huge knight, virtually a giant, who gives off an air of threat and menace to the assembled nobles. He appears as the monstrous wild man of the woods, imbued with a hideous strength and power. In a booming voice, the intruder challenged the knights to a "Christmas game." He will exchange blows with any champion in the hall on the understanding that whoever gives him a blow will accept a blow in return. This will continue until one defeats the other. The interloper looks so powerful and menacing that most of the knights shy away from his challenge, but Gawain alone agrees to enter the contest. Although fearsome looking, the giant knight is soon defeated, and in triumph Gawain lops off his head using his own axe. However, to the horror of those around, the monstrous knight does not die but simply gathers up his head and holds it aloft, allowing it to survey the assembled host. The horrid voice now tells them that although the knight appears defeated, he can still deliver a return blow for the one Gawain has given him. In order to receive this, as was agreed, Gawain must journey to the

Green Chapel where, within a year, the Green Knight will deliver the return blow. In order to honor his agreement, Gawain immediately mounts his horse and sets off to look for the Green Chapel, leaving his comrades stunned behind him.

This first part of the text sets the scene and draws upon many of the folkloric elements of the Green Man. The giant knight undoubtedly represents the natural elements and the wildness and strength of Nature. As with the King of the Wood, he allows himself to be sacrificed for his people, but only if his slayer will submit to the same sacrifice in a year's time. This may represent a reciprocal process—attempting to reunify man with Nature by humans taking on some of the aspects of the Forest King. The timing of the fable is also significant—the fight is conducted near Christmastime as winter takes hold on the world; the mysterious knight may be the last vestige of the green world, dying so that spring may live again.

In the second part of the text, Sir Gawain sets out on his quest to find the Green Chapel (perhaps suggestive of Nature itself and of Mankind's reunion with it). Eventually, he arrives at the forbidding castle of Sir Bercilak, a somewhat fierce and hearty nobleman. Bercilak assures Gawain that the Chapel he is seeking is near at hand and offers to go there with him when the day of combat comes. Reassured, Gawain settles down to enjoy the lord's hospitality. Each day, Bercilak goes hunting, returning with a wide variety of animals that he has killed in the forest. A strange bargain is set up between the two men. Sir Bercilak will give Gawain all that he has caught in the forest and in return Gawain will give him all that he has caught at home. Once again, the notion of the reciprocal exchange comes into play. Gawain fully expects to gain nothing at home with which he can trade but each morning, after her husband has departed for the hunt, Bercilak's beautiful wife enters his chamber and offers herself to him. Of all Arthur's knights, Gawain is credited as being the finest lover, and doubtless the lady wished to test this out for herself. However, Gawain is a knight and is bound by a code of courtly conduct. This makes him refuse her advances, but he allows her a chaste kiss on his cheek, which he then gives to Bercilak each evening when he returns from hunting. This curious exchange occurs three times, but fearing his own death at the hands of the Green Knight, Gawain finds it harder and harder to resist the lady's advances. At last, she persuades him to accept a gift—a green baldric that she assures him will magically protect him from the Knight in the Green Chapel. Eventually the day dawns and Gawain prepares to go and meet the Knight. Bercilak does not accompany Gawain himself but sends a guide to take him to the Green Chapel. The Chapel turns out to be little more than a hillock by the side of a river ford with an entrance and exit through the bushes. Here Gawain walks around, awaiting his opponent. The Green Knight suddenly appears—as menacing and terrifying as his original intrusion—and Gawain kneels to receive the promised blow. Twice his adversary moves to make the blow and twice he draws back. On a third attempt, he mocks Gawain's foolish courage, but Gawain is unmoved. Finally, the Green Knight nicks Gawain's neck, drawing blood, and declares himself satisfied. Then, to Gawain's astonishment, the Green Knight reveals himself to be Sir Bercilak, who has been placed under a spell by King Arthur's sorcerous sister, Morgaine (Morgana le Fay). Indeed, Gawain has already met with the enchantress in Bercilak's castle where she appears as an ugly old woman whom he mistakes as a servant. The entire adventure has been arranged by Morgaine to test the courage of her brother's court and that of Sir Gawain in particular. He has passed the test save in one respect—he feared Death so much that he accepted the baldric from Sir Bercilak's wife, hoping that it would protect him—hence the wound on his neck. With the test now concluded, Gawain returns to Camelot to be feted as a hero.

Some students of early English literature have suggested that the second part of the text may have been added later but it is clear that the fable, or something similar to it, was circulating much earlier than the 1300s. Indeed, this may be a "modern" adaptation of an old legend from Celtic mythology and folklore.

The two figures of the Green Knight and Sir Bercilak are possibly a variant of the mysterious Cú Rói mac Dáire who appears in the ancient Irish epic, the *Fled Bricriu* (Bricriu's Feast), which is part of the great Ulster Cycle. Cú Rói appears to be a mysterious character, as it is difficult to distinguish what is legend and what is history from the stories about him. He may well have been an actual historical figure, thought to have been a king of Munster possibly at a time between the Bronze and Iron Ages. According to some legends, he had strong connections with the Tuatha dé Danann (fairy people in Ireland who represent the gods) and may well have had some supernatural blood coursing through his veins. He was certainly a mighty warrior, fabled for a number of exploits, which he is said to have achieved by supernatural means, given his fairy origins.

At a great feast conducted by the warriors of Ulster, Cú Rói appears, disguised as a giant, very much in the style of the Green Knight, and offers to play a game—known as the Beheading Game—with any warrior who accepts his challenge. Three heroes, Conall Cearnach (a Knight of the Red Branch), Laughairre, and

Cu Cuhulainn (the Hound of Ulster) agree to play the game with him. Whoever wins is to be acknowledged as the greatest champion in all of Ireland. The "game" consists of each of the heroes cutting off Cú Rói's head, in return for allowing him to do the same to them. Thinking that after the first beheading, Cú Rói will be in no position to retaliate, both Conall and Laughairre strike their blows, but each time Cú Rói simply lifts the fallen head and replaces it on his shoulders. Terrified, Conall and Laughairre flee the hall, leaving Cu Cuhulainn to face Cú Rói on his own. He prepares to take the return blow but Cú Rói only taps him lightly on the neck, grazing the skin only slightly with the edge of his axe. He then declares Cu Cuhulainn to be the bravest man in all of Ireland and worthy of the champion's portion at the feast. Only later is it revealed that the giant is none other that Cú Rói, and that he has been testing the greatest heroes in Ireland.

Cú Rói was unwise to spare Cu Cuhulainn, for the Ulster hero would be the one who would later slay him after plotting with his lover Blathnat who is, in the fable, one of the Tuatha dé Danann.

In these stories (and one may be a variant of the other), both the Green Knight and Cú Rói mac Dáire appear in disguise—in both cases as giants or as wild men. An ancient Celtic word for giant or ogre is *bachlach*—although in Celtic mythology this name is often more specifically applied to the ancient Fomorian giant who dwelt in a glass tower on Tory Island off the coast of County Donegal in Ireland. And it has been pointed out that this appears similar to the name Bercilek in the tale of *Sir Gawain and the Green Knight,* thus closely identifying the wild giant with the Green Man (or Green Knight).

However, the involvement of Sir Gawain in the Green Man legends does not end there. One of the more popular poems from the late medieval period was one known as *The Wedding of Sir Gawain and Dame Ragnell* or *The Loathly Lady*. As with the story of the Green Knight, the author of this text is uncertain, and it may have been extensively added to over the Middle Ages.

This tale directly involves King Arthur himself. While out hunting deep in the forest, the monarch becomes separated from his men. Nevertheless, he kills a stag but is confronted by a hostile knight named Gromer who threatens to kill him. Arthur pleads for an opportunity to save himself, and the other considers his request. He then issues a quest-riddle. Arthur must find what it is that every woman most desires—a seemingly impossible task. And the king must return with the answer within a year. Shaken and baffled, Arthur returns to Camelot and reveals the puzzle to his knights who are sent out to find the answer. He commissions Sir Gawain, who is now described as his nephew, to take command of the search.

With Gawain, Arthur sets out on a search across his kingdom, questioning every woman they meet and receiving a different answer every time, all of which are recorded in a great book. Entering a deep wood and close to the end of the stipulated year, Arthur meets a hideously ugly woman at a woodland crossroads, who mysteriously knows of his quest and who offers to give him an answer that will satisfy Gromer. She calls herself Ragnell (or Ragnall) and says that she has a "special knowledge" of what Gromer might want. There is a condition, however. If she reveals the answer, the king must instruct Gawain, his companion, to marry her. Gawain is the most eligible of all the knights and the ugly woman desires that he become her husband.

Terrified that Gromer will kill him, Arthur reluctantly agrees, giving his word that he will so instruct his nephew. He meets with Gromer and hands him the book of answers, which he hopes will satisfy him. Gromer, however, rejects all the answers. Arthur then offers the answer that Ragnell has given—that every woman desires sovereignty. Gromer flies into a great rage—only one person could have known that answer, his sister Ragnell. However, true to his word, he spares Arthur's life.

Relieved at his escape but sad for his nephew who must now marry the hideous crone, Arthur returns to Camelot. Commanded by his sovereign, Gawain has no other option but to agree to the match. The pair are married in some grandeur, although Gawain's wedding is said to break the heart of every woman in the kingdom. He takes the ugly woman to the bridal chamber where the hideous bride asks her husband for a passionate kiss. Although the sight of her almost makes him ill, Gawain agrees and kisses her in a lingering embrace. Almost at once, the hideous female turns into a beautiful young woman in his arms. She explains that both she and Gromer have been placed under a spell by Morgana le Fay. However, the spell is not completely broken, for Gawain has yet another choice to make. He can choose to have his wife as a beautiful woman by day and an ugly woman by night or vice versa. Unable to make up his mind and always chivalrous and courteous, Gawain asks Ragnell to choose, because it is she who will be most affected by the decision. At this, the lady claps her hands in delight and announces that the spell is now completely broken. By such an act of selflessness, he has thrown off Morgana le Fay's enchantment and from then on Ragnell would remain young and beautiful. She then reveals the truth of her answer to Gawain—women most desire the sovereignty over who they will be.

The tale is most unusual; it is virtually unique amongst medieval legends, and differs from the previous tales in one particular but fundamental aspect: that the central figure in this case is a woman. It also differs in that the solution is reached, not by force of arms or by physical courage, but through care and thoughtfulness. However, this may be one of the few instances in folklore in which the Green Man becomes the Green Woman. This has led some folklorists to speculate that this version of the story comes from a much later time than the previous two—a time when women were becoming aware of themselves and of their status within society. Nevertheless, some of the old folkloric motifs are still there.

Ragnell is, in the first instance, a drab and ugly woman, perhaps symbolizing winter and the sterile earth. Through the selflessness of her husband, she becomes transformed into what might be described as the Spring Maiden—the symbol of flourishing Nature. There are too the symbols of the quest and the challenge, albeit portrayed in a much different context from the previous legends. The quest is for the reunion of Man and Nature, symbolized by the recognizable image of a wedding.

However, Ragnell also represents the darker and wilder side of Nature—she is hideously ugly even to the point of being repellent. In some traditions, her voice is described as being "harsh and unpleasant," and she is certainly not a desirable female. And yet, working with her husband and showing love from him, she is transformed into an image of beauty. The fable, it might be argued, underlines a yearning for Man to be restored as part of Nature, and to be returned to that state that he had lost. No matter how dark or unpleasant Nature can be, that urge is still there.

Many of these characters, of course, may well be far older than the medieval period and may in fact come, as we have seen, from ancient Celtic legend and folklore. Indeed, many later folktales from places such as Ireland, Scotland, Wales, and Cornwall seem to have been based upon similar origins. Some of these have been handed down into comparatively modern times. For example, a story of three sons who set out to make their fortune in the world is a recurrent theme in such folktales. In several of these, interest usually focuses on the youngest, who has to perform a series of tasks or follow a quest at the instruction of an ogre or magician in order to win a prize or the hand of a beautiful girl (in many cases, the king's daughter). In a number of such stories too, the lady turns out to be rather ugly, but when faced with true love, becomes radiantly beautiful. Once again, such tales show the strength of Mankind's deep-seated longing to reunite with the natural world, born in earliest times, continuing down through the medieval and early modern times to manifest itself in much more recent times.

The Green Man, then, becomes a physical defender of Nature and of the Natural ways. Moreover, in this role, he becomes a setter of tests and quests (whether physical or spiritual) to determine whether individuals are worthy of a compatibility with the Natural world. The face that looks out from amongst the foliage is a wary watcher, ready to turn away or test any intruder. But there is yet more to the image.

The Guardian of Knowledge

In the medieval mind the Green Man was probably also seen as a guardian of *knowledge*, which was deemed to have been lost in the separation between Man and Nature. Gradually, a perception was dawning upon men that, although they were probably more "sophisticated" than they had been before, they had formerly been privy to the secrets of the Natural world that were now lost to them. The Green Man was now the protector of that knowledge and would only release it to those who were deemed worthy. In many of the folktales originating in the period, a hero often meets an old man or an old woman deep in the forest who imparts great knowledge to him or else gives him a magical artifact, which he can use in a task or quest. In this case, the Green Man (or Green Woman) becomes the repository or defender of a knowledge or secret, which is unknown to Mankind, and which possibly comes from an older time.

Throughout the medieval period, there were many searches for such "hidden secrets" that would unlock the mysteries of Nature: the Philosopher's Stone, which could transform base metals into pure gold; the Emerald Tablet, which if ground down and consumed in a measure of wine would enable the drinker to live forever, and various other sundry "secrets." In fact, it was claimed that some of these mysteries had been revealed to certain selected individuals or groups who then kept such knowledge for themselves.

The Knights Templar

The medieval military order known as the Knights Templar was one of these groups, and they allegedly bore a direct connection to the Green Man. One of the connections is the 15th century Rosslyn

Chapel near Edinburgh in Scotland, which has been made famous by both the book and film *The Da Vinci Code*. Although not strictly a Templar church—it was built in 1446, more than a hundred years after the disintegration of the Order—it is still associated with them and with the older mysteries they embodied. Although there are many mysterious carvings at Rosslyn, amongst them is a Green Man with foliage issuing from the corner of his mouth. This image, it has been hinted, is one of the central mysteries of the ornate chapel.

The Knights Templar was an order of religious knights that came into existence in the Middle East during the First Crusade (1095–1099). Essentially, they had been formed to protect pilgrims on their way to Christian shrines in the Holy Land that had been won back from the Islamic Saracens. Although these holy places were now theoretically open to Christians, Muslim raiders still lurked along the way, proving to be a threat and a menace to those who travelled there. The Order of Poor Fellow-Soldiers of Christ and the Temple of Solomon, to give them their full title, grew from a number of pious soldiers who had gathered in Jerusalem during the second decade of the 12th century. They began by protecting the roads around the important port of Jaffa where military ships were landing, but later extended their influence towards the city of Jerusalem, which had been captured by the Crusaders. In 1118, during the reign of the Christian king of Jerusalem, Baldwin II, seven of the holy knights, together with their leader Hughes de Payens and Godfrey St. Omer presented themselves before the Patriarch of Jerusalem to take a vow of poverty and service. Baldwin accepted their vow and assigned them to guard the lands around Jerusalem, assigning them the Temple Mount (believed to be the ruins of the

Temple of Solomon) as their headquarters. This would give the Order its name—the Templars.

The Templars were soon a rather controversial order. Having been formed by French knights, they soon expanded across the Holy Land and beyond. A largely monastic order, they also became involved in a number of areas, including financial ones (they looked after the valuables of pilgrims, thus guarding against robbery). They were extremely secretive and it was rumored that admission to the Order was through a number of tests and ceremonies. Although recognized by the Church, they were largely autonomous and the Order was largely under the control of Masters who presided over the various Templar houses; there was also a Grand Master in France. This earned them the enmity of several other orders and their financial dealings—especially in the affairs of various countries— and did not endear them to particular monarchs. The first king to move against the Order was Philip IV of France, who was deeply in debt to the Templars; he persuaded the French pope, Clement V, to denounce the whole Templar movement. Rumors had been circulating about the Order for some time, much of them rather fantastic and speculative.

It was said, for example, that the Order protected "great mysteries," which was the reason for its secrecy. Many of these "mysteries" were allegedly brought back from the Holy Land and were said to include the bones of Christ, a particular goat-headed idol, and a representation of the Black Virgin. Most of these had allegedly been found beneath the ruins of Solomon's Temple. It was also widely rumored that the Templars had brought back a head of brass, which they venerated. This head spoke at certain times of the day and divulged the secrets of the Universe to those who uttered certain incantations. This head of brass would later be changed into the mummified head of Christ Himself. Also, the Templars were alleged to have learned "many secrets of Nature" from the Arabs, secrets that they brought back to Europe with them. None of this was ever proven, but the rumors were enough to turn much of Christendom against them, and in 1305, Philip IV ordered the burning of the Grand French Master, Jacques de Molay, and the seizure of Templar assets. Urged on by the French king, Pope Clement denounced the Templars as heretics. This gave many Western monarchs the opportunity to rid themselves of their debt to the Order by seizing their lands, monasteries, and churches. Although the Templars were formally excised, it is said that their influence lived on and manifests itself today in Freemasonry. This brings us to the famous chapel near Edinburgh.

Rosslyn Chapel

Work on Rosslyn started in 1446, under the direct instructions of William St. Clair, the last of the St. Clair Princes of Orkney. Although the Templar Order had been formally dissolved in 1312, rumors persisted that it still survived in a fragmented form through the medieval and early modern periods, and that it continued to guard the mysteries it had obtained in the Eastern lands. It was thought that Sir William might be a form of Templar and that he might have access to the esoteric "knowledge" with which the Order had been connected. Certainly, he took a great interest in Rosslyn Chapel's construction, detailing exactly how it was to be laid out and what elaborate carvings were to be included. It was suggested that Rosslyn, in common with many earlier Templar churches, was built along ancient natural channels of power in the landscape known as ley lines, which harnessed Natural forces that could then be used for supernatural purposes by learned mages and sorcerers. The construction of such buildings was usually done to a precise geometric pattern in order to contain the energies that flowed through them, and it has been suggested that this is why St. Clair was so specific about how Rosslyn was to be built. It is also thought that he may have envisaged a greater building—a kind of natural "power house"—than the one that was finally constructed.

The site he had chosen for the church was in a glen that had a reputation as being a center of Druid worship (it has even been suggested that it was the location of an underground temple of the Eastern entity Mithras), and this added greatly to the idea that it was to be the center of Natural energies. Sir William's interest in the building took on almost fanatical proportions—in draft form, he inspected *every* carving to be included. He also imported, at huge expense, stonemasons from both France and Italy so that these carvings could be done *precisely* to his specifications. It was said that he was following old Templar plans that had been laid out by the Master of the main Scottish Templar houses, Brian de Jay, who had sold the Scottish Order out to the English king Edward I in 1291.

One of the carvings was of a Green Man, and it appears that Sir William had decided that this was to be a somewhat central figure. It was thought to have been envisaged as the focal point of earthly forces, which would be channeled through other figures and symbols within the building. The foliage that ran from the corner of its mouth was to extend around various parts of the Chapel, thus giving the carving a kind of centrality. For some reason this was never completed, and so the carving simply remains as a face with foliage emerging from the side of its mouth. It now exists amongst other religious and quasi-Pagan figures, which also adorn the ancient chapel. Sir William specifically wished this carving to be included as an acknowledgement of Rosslyn's Celtic and Druidic past, though some have argued that this was to be the central point of the ancient ley lines, which were supposed to run through the glen. The Chapel took 40 years to build and was counted as one of the most architecturally spectacular, if somewhat mysterious, buildings outside Edinburgh.

Rosslyn was lavishly endowed by Sir William and by his grandson, also called Sir William, in 1523. The latter Sir William also built living accommodation, in the locality and farmed the lands around the area. However, by the late 16th century, the times were changing in Scotland. Protestantism was now taking hold and the St. Clairs (or Sinclairs as they now styled themselves) had remained staunchly Catholic, much to the enmity of many of their neighbors. Following the English Civil War, the Cromwellians entered Scotland, determined to subdue its populace and root out Catholicism. General George Monck attacked Rosslyn Chapel in 1650 and used the chapel as a stable for his horses. Although many such churches in the area were destroyed, Rosslyn was miraculously spared. Some have suggested that this was because Monck (later Lord Albemarle) used the place to restore ordnance to his troops, but others have hinted that it may have been because of the significance of the site, and because Oliver Cromwell himself was secretly an early Freemason.

But Rosslyn's troubles were not over. On December 11, 1688, the chapel was attacked once more by a Protestant mob from Rosslyn Chapel who believed it to be a "sorcerous place," and that local Witches were gathering there to do great evil.

Interestingly enough, the now abandoned ruins of Rosslyn Chapel came to prominence again around 1717 when plans were made to partially rebuild the church. One of the reasons for doing the restoration in 1717 was that the English Freemasons were founded around the same time. James St. Clair was prompted by Sir John Clerk of Penicuik to restore the building to at least part of its former glory. The repairs were completed in 1736, the very year in which the Scottish Lodge of Freemasons was founded. In fact, Sir William St. Clair became the first Grand Master of the Lodge in that same year. This strengthened the perception of linkages between the Green Man and the guardians of esoteric knowledge (as the early Freemasons were perceived to be). The geometric construction of the church, the placing and precise carvings of the ornamentation and the alleged associations with former Pagan worship all point to some plan that involved Natural forces. Through Rosslyn, the associations between the Green Man, the Templars, and the Freemasons seemed very clear. Some of these connections will be examined in more detail later in this book.

The history of the Green Man is a long and complicated one, stretching from the earliest Celtic times, through the Middle Ages and perhaps to the very origins of Freemasonry. Much of that history had been rooted in the early Celtic and Christian mythology and lore. However, both as an image and as an ideal, the Green Man has a much wider pedigree than that—the knowing, ancient face that peers out from amongst the foliage is not solely a Celtic one. And so it is to other representations of the same (or rather similar) figure in other places and cultures that we now turn.

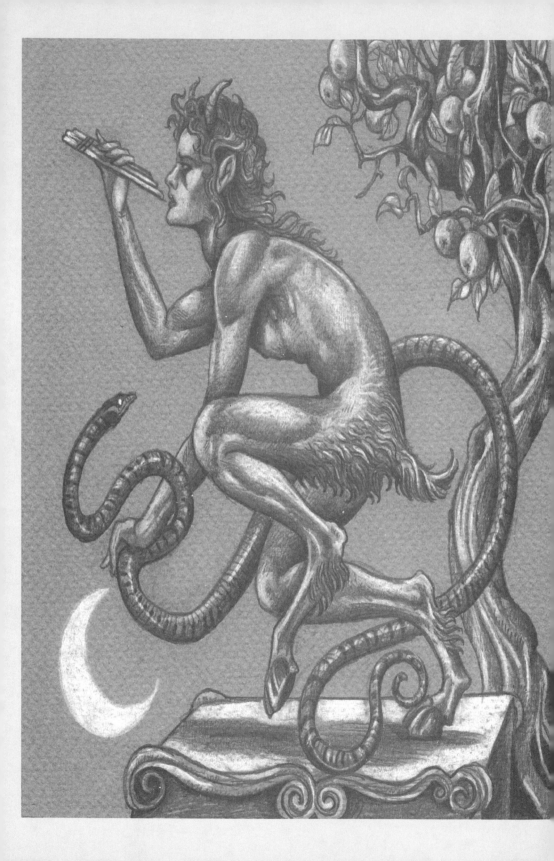

Chapter 3

Echoes From the East

There are many images and impressions associated with the Green Man. Amongst these are English pub signs, festivals and dancing in an English village, and the ancient ruined churches and monasteries in parts of Western Europe. In fact, it has almost become something of an English or British ideal. We could be forgiven, therefore, for assuming that the Green Man was a purely European image, and moreover was largely confined to the west of that continent. We could also mistakenly assume that it emerged out of Celtic culture alone. This, of course, is far from the truth, for the Green Man (or something similar to him) appears in a number of other cultures, particularly those further east.

If the seasons and the cycles of growth and crops were important to the Celts, they were equally so to other ancient peoples. From earliest times, communities have depended upon the certainty of their harvests for their very survival. A poor harvest could mean the extinction of an entire village, town, or city in those distant days, and so every means should be taken to ensure growth in abundance throughout the year.

Ancient Sumer: The Roles of Enki and Yahweh

Through the *Epic of Gilgamesh,* we have already noted the notion of wildness in early Sumerian society. The Sumerian god of fertility and of growing things was Enki, son of Anu, the sky god. Although originally thought to have been a water god, Enki quickly became associated with growth and vegetation, and it is not hard to see why because water is linked to growth and fertility. It was said to have been Enki who created Man in a "Mound of Creation" and also who saved Humankind from a mighty flood that covered the Earth. Scoured by the great and turbulent waters, the Earth was barren and desolate. So, to save his creation—Man—Enki covered it with a carpet of green and growing things. He also bestowed upon Man the knowledge to draw the best from these growths. In fact, he became in his own way, a kind of Green Man, ruling creation through the functioning of Humankind. He was also strongly connected with the idea of the cycle of death and rebirth in all natural things. Enki may have been one of a number of early deities associated with growth, fertility, and death, who were worshipped by prehistoric man and whose names have probably been lost to us forever.

Indeed, Yahweh (Jehovah) might have initially been such a god, charged as Enki was, with the reforestation of the Earth after some mythological catastrophe. One of God's earliest commands to Adam and Eve in Genesis was "Be fruitful and multiply and *replenish* (refill) the earth." The use of the word "replenish" here is both interesting and significant because it suggests refilling, repopulation, and renewal. The inference to be taken is that the Earth has been populated before, but this is now gone, the Earth is in need of rebirth, and this is central to God's instruction. The command, of course, has been frequently retranslated and may have meant something else, but it does, on the face of it, fit in with some of the notions concerning other long-vanished gods. However, the ideal of death and rebirth continued to survive in the human mind.

Egyptian Mythology

Osiris

We have also seen how this ideal was transferred into Egyptian mythology in the person of the god Osiris. It is thought that the perception of Osiris probably grew out of the alternating flooding and cultivation of the Nile Delta and that this was taken to be the cycle of life and of growth that the god presided over. The growth of green crops after the flood was certainly symbolic of the rising of life after destruction and death, and signaled the god's return to the world to protect and look after his people. To represent the death and resurrection of Osiris, it is said that mummy cases (the symbols of death) were filled with grains and seeds, then left out in the rain so that the seeds would sprout into green shoots, which were the symbol of life.

Nut

Within this symbolic cycle, Osiris was said to "become" Horus, the son of his union with the goddess Isis. Horus himself was protected by a serpent known as Wadjet, which was said to be the color of papyrus. Horus may also have had a green element, which he had inherited from his mother. Indeed, in some aspects of early Egyptian mythology, the color green was associated with eternal femininity, perhaps giving rise to the concept of a Green Woman. This may also be the representation of an even older goddess known as Nut. Nut was the goddess of the starry heavens, she also represented the quick, green life that rose out of the womb of the Watery Abyss— perhaps another symbol of the rising and flooding Nile and the fertile land that was to emerge from it after the waters had receded. Indeed, in an extremely ancient text roughly translated as the *Myth of Noah* (which is given as Semite but may be partly Egyptian), the patriarch Noah, adrift in a small boat, invokes the sky goddess to aid him in finding land as the Great Flood appears to recede; she sends him a green shoot in the beak of a fowl as her symbol. This may well be the basis for the Biblical story of Noah's Ark. The fertile land that Noah inherits is too much for him and he becomes intoxicated on his own produce (his grapes, which make wine) and finishes his days as a drunkard, overwhelmed by the forces of Nature he sought to control.

Hathor

The ancient Egyptians also worshipped a powerful goddess, one aspect of whom was a tree. This was Hathor, who appears in some early tomb paintings. She was closely connected to the sycamore where she made her home, and from which she often fed those who had recently died and wanted to receive sustenance. This connects her to the Green Man and to the notions of death, rebirth, and renewal. It also serves as a connection with trees and tree deities stretching back into early Egypt.

Ancient Greeks

Dryads

The Egyptians were not the only ancient civilization to connect their gods with the woodlands and with Nature. Amongst the ancient Greeks, for instance, there was a widespread belief in *dryads*, or tree creatures. The name comes from the Greek word *drys* signifying oak, which in turn comes from the older Indo-European root word "*derew(o)*" meaning wood or thicket. This same root also connected the Celtic Druids with the oak (their name meant "men of the oak") and provided a link between Humankind and the Natural world, especially trees. The Druids allegedly drew part of their special powers through rituals conducted at certain trees, usually oak. To the Greek mind, dryads were spirits, usually female, who were the humanlike manifestation of such trees and who often lived within them or amongst their branches. They had an ambivalent nature— either acting kindly towards travelers who rested in the shade of their branches, or killing them. There was even a species of them known as hamadryads, who were attached to specific trees and protected them. These creatures would certainly kill anyone who did damage to the growths with which they were connected. Indeed, so closely connected were they that if the tree were to die or be cut down, the dryad would also die and the gods might take revenge upon Mankind for the act of negligence. In many instances, the Greeks

A dryad

believed that these creatures were best avoided because of their capricious nature. They were often regarded as tricksters, luring men deep into the forests in the guise of beautiful or voluptuous women, and then either killing them or leaving them to wander along the forest trails until they died from exhaustion and hunger. Most dryads, while exceptionally beautiful, were also dangerous and hostile towards Mankind.

The Celts and The English

The Oakmen

Amongst other ancient peoples, the dryads had male counterparts. These were little men who dwelt either in the trees themselves or amongst their roots. The Scottish Celts knew them as *Bodach na Criobhe Moire*—the Old Man of the Great Tree—and they were feared all over the Scottish countryside. These were also known as Oakmen in parts of northern England, although the trees with which they were associated were not necessarily oaks. The Oakmen were usually described as small, gnarled, and ugly men about the height of a 2-year-old child. They were viewed as protectors of the trees with which they were associated, and were generally regarded as incredibly hostile toward humans. The use of the Celtic word *bodach* is interesting here. The word certainly means "old man"—usually a senile old man—but it can also mean "clown" in reference to an incompetent person or a trickster. In fact, the Oakmen, akin to the dryads, were something of a danger to humans through their malicious pranks and tricks. In the forests their power was absolute, and they could and would often mislead travelers through the forests by manipulating the paths and woodland trails. This trickery amused them greatly. Another of their "jests" was to place scrumptious-looking fungi in the way of country folk as they passed through the wood and then poison it when it was gathered, cooked, and eaten. In this way, some of their "jokes" turned out to be fatal. The Oakmen not only protected the trees of the forest but also guarded a great hoard of treasure that had been deposited somewhere in the woodland depths in some former time—perhaps during Viking days. The gnarled and wizened face of the Oakman peered out from amongst the roadside foliage or the overhanging branches of trees—watchful and wary, ready for those upon whom he could play his tricks. This may have been a precursor to our image of the Green Man.

Although the Oakman was largely a Celtic image, and appears in the folklore of both Scotland and the north of England, this did not prevent other cultures from having similar figures or from adapting the same ideal. The early Germanic peoples, for example, incorporated these creatures into their notion of *kobolds*—small, malignant dwarves who dwelt in the deep woods or underground. Initially, kobolds were miners, but in later folktales they became woodsmen or forest dwellers, living deep in the woodlands. In popular tales they lived well away from humans and had very little to do with them except to trick them from time to time. In some cases, the idea of the Oakmen, spirits of the trees, became integrated with the Germanic *Alp,* a kind of vampire. Alps would fall upon passing travelers (usually from the branches of their trees), kill them, and lap up their blood like dogs. There was little defence against them. Again their faces peered out from amongst the foliage, seeking out possible victims; this may be the origin of the Green Man head as it appears in Germanic lands.

The Romans

Satyrs

The Romans too had notions of wild creatures living in the deep forests. These, as has already been mentioned, were part man and part animal. Usually they had the upper torso of a human being and the lower hindquarters of a goat, and were known as satyrs. These were shaggy, uncouth beings, covered in a mat of dark hair suggesting a wild and untamed nature. Tiny horns grew from their heads, perhaps reminiscent of the antlers of the early Shamans or the leaders of the Wild Hunt. They were also earthy, hedonistic woodland entities who were continually drunken and lecherous. Indeed the word *satyr* is now used to describe some persons of questionable sexual and hedonistic appetites. The chief deity amongst them was known as Pan or Bacchus. In his Greek form, as we have seen, Bacchus was known as Dionysus. As with many other ancient Nature beings, the satyrs were lords of the forest; this was where they congregated for drunken debaucheries and revels. And, in the gloomy shade under the trees, they carried out unspeakable drunken orgies. These beliefs were viewed with such disdain and alarm by the early Christian Church that the cloven hoof (the symbol of the goat and of the satyr) became incorporated into Christian mythology and folklore as the unmistakable mark of the Devil. In fact, the idea of the Enemy of Mankind was forged out of the idea of the satyrs. Amongst the early Christian, here emerges a composite figure—half man, half beast—but always with the cloven hoof. This, to the ancient Roman mind, was also the mark of the satyr, the spirit of the woodlands, and was strongly connected with Nature and the Natural world. Satan also had horns, possibly the remnant of the ancient crown of antlers, symbolic of Nature worship. Thus the goat-man became a kind of evil symbol, a figure of lust and depravity. The shaggy, bearded, knowing head of the satyr might serve as a template for the foliage-shrouded head of the Green Man.

But as with everything else about the Green Man, the satyrs had a dual nature. They were in fact marvellous musicians and could extract the most beautiful and haunting melodies from reed pipes—later known as Pan pipes after the Roman satyr-god. The satyrs were also wonderful composers, creating eerily wistful melodies that could be played upon their reed pipes. This aspect softened their debauched image slightly and turned the lecherous satyrs into the more acceptable fauns—also goat-footed half-men. They were the companions and followers of the Roman god Faunus who seemed to be a later and less wild incarnation of Pan. Fauns are exemplified by the gentle Mr. Tumnus in C.S. Lewis's *The Lion, the Witch and the Wardrobe* (recently filmed as *The Chronicles of Narnia*), a good soul who can be corrupted by the evil around him. But beneath this more benign and "civilized" face, the shadow of the satyr still lurked.

Goat-Footed Races and Tales in Western Europe

Goat-footed creatures living in wild and often inaccessible places occur in many folktales across Western Europe. Some of these legends may actually predate the coming of Christianity. A number of folktales, mainly from Europe, refer to goat-footed races, which may have predated Mankind, still living in remote parts of the country. In the Brocken Mountains in Germany for example, goat-footed beings lured young girls away into the inaccessible, forest-lined valleys, never to be seen again. In some stories, heroes ventured forth to try and bring them back, but they got lost and never returned. In parts of Scandinavia, there are tales of King Herla, who encountered a goat-footed king while out hunting deep in the forest. This goat-footed king was the last remnant of an ancient tribe, which had existed in the woodlands before the coming of Man. The goat-footed king invited Herla to his wedding, which was a sumptuous, if Pagan, affair, and extracted a promise from Herla that he would return the favor one day. Upon his return to his own kingdom, Herla soon forgot about the promise, and some years after, was betrothed to a beautiful but intensely religious princess. His own wedding was a grand affair conducted by an archbishop in the Christian Church with many churchmen present. As they sat down to eat, word reached Herla that a procession of small, goat-footed men had emerged from the forest and that their king was seeking an invitation to the banquet. Herla remembered his promise but was ashamed that he had been associated with these Pagan creatures. Moreover, he was frightened that his new bride and the assembled churchmen would meet these brings and would revile him for consorting with Pagans. So, he instructed his guards to turn them away.

Some time later, Herla was hunting in the forest once more when he encountered the goat-footed king lurking in the bushes. The king greeted him cheerfully but reminded him that he had not fulfilled his promise. Nevertheless, he had brought a present for Herla that he had intended to give him on his wedding day, but which he would give to him now. The present turned out to be a small dog, which jumped into Herla's arms and would not get down. Herla then found that he could not dismount from his horse and neither could the men who were with him. The goat-footed king then told them that they would ride forever through the forest until he chose to recall the dog or until the Great Day of Judgment—whichever came first. Thus, Herla and his company were condemned forever to ride through the Scandinavian forests, at the beck and call of the goat-footed king and his people. Strangely, although this is ostensibly a Scandinavian story, it also occurs in some parts of Ireland, particularly in the north, and may have been due to Viking influence.

In the story of Herla and his warriors endlessly riding through the forest, we find echoes of the Wild Hunt, and in the character of the goat-footed king who condemns Herla to his fate, we may also find some elements of the Green Man. This is representative of a far older race than Man and, in a sense, is the essential spirit of Nature and of the forest itself. The ancient entity takes over the life of Herla, who has shunned it, and condemns him to an awful existence. In some ancient tales, the passing of Herla and his followers signaled and warned of an approaching storm—thus, in one respect, Herla was actually *serving* Natural ends and was inextricably connected to Natural events.

The Goat-Footed Race in Eastern Europe

The goat-footed figure is, however, not confined to the lost or fairy races of Western Europe. In Eastern Europe too, it makes a similar and dreadful appearance—usually as a stranger or traveler, whose motives are often malign, arriving out of the wilderness to take part in some sort of community activity. Country people gathered for a local dance in the village square or on some lonely spot are joined by a tall and extremely handsome man wearing obviously expensive clothes. However, he walks somewhat oddly as he crosses to the most beautiful girl at the gathering and asks her to dance with him. She dances with him but as she looks down, she sees the cloven hoof and recognizes him as the Devil or an evil spirit from the forest or mountains nearby. In another variant of the tale, some gamblers are playing cards when they are joined by a stranger who asks if he might also play. When he does, he keeps winning, depriving them of most of their money. Then, one of the players accidentally drops his cards, and stooping to retrieve them, he sees that the stranger has cloven feet. In this way, Nature intrudes on human activity in a humanized form.

Okeanus

The Greek figure of Dionysus/Pan therefore underwent many changes as it spread Westward across Europe. Amongst some of the tribes there, he also assumed a Shamanistic role—a creature of prophesy and healing. He was also represented as Lord of the Animals to whom even the wildest of creatures was subservient. His name, in this instance, was Okeanus and he was often represented simply as a bearded head, usually surrounded by foliage. Here again, the idea of water, growth, and renewal are paramount, for the name Okeanus is thought to be of an Indo-European root-word meaning a body of water or mighty river; this is where we get our word *ocean*. The idea of Okeanus as a head-figure is supposedly the humanized representation of a great river that encircled the world. This was, in

Egyptian mythology "the primordial waters" out of which the world rose and to which every living thing was connected. The idea of a verdant land rising out of the waters of the Flood appears in many ancient mythologies, but was especially potent to the Egyptians because it was believed that the Nile flowed out of the sea, through their lands, and back to the ocean again, thus forming a kind of loop or circle. The head of Okeanus represented that circle.

In ancient Egypt, the face of Okeanus was known as "the Great Green" and represented verdant fertility. It was believed that the deity had emerged from the River of Life and that his touch had reinvigorated the world, creating life, which had risen from out of the Primal Waters. Thus, Okeanus was both a renewer and creator, bestowing life and vitality, and may have been contemporaneous to the Dionysus/Pan entity.

Smoke and Air

In the Middle East, however, Natural forces took a slightly different aspect—although there were still attempts to humanize them. So far, we have talked about such elements as vegetation and water, but for the early Semites, the Natural entities were usually things of smoke and air. Although insubstantial in Nature, they nonetheless represented the same aspects of wildness and unpredictability, which were evidenced by their Western European counterparts. They dwelt in remote and isolated (often inaccessible) places, they were capricious in temperament, and they sometimes demonstrated their will through destruction and renewal. They often manifested themselves as pillars of clouds or as fearsome winds, out in desert areas or in forests on the lower slopes of mountain regions. They could flatten crops, they carried dust and sand that polluted the rivers and streams, and yet, they also brought rain, which was essential for making things grow. This, once again, was the cycle of destruction and later renewal and rebirth, which appeared to be evident everywhere within Nature. Such cloud pillars could be beneficent—as the pillar that guided the Children of Israel through their 40 years wandering in the wilderness, but they could also be violent and destructive as the great whirlwinds that devastated towns and cities.

The idea of insubstantial, cloudy entities did, of course, not sit well with humans and soon there was an attempt to "humanize" them and make them more accessible to those who worshipped them. There seemed to be nothing more human than a face—it was the face, after all, which gave every individual his or her unique identity. It was also, through expression and word, the way humans themselves communicated with each other. The face might also suggest thought and intelligence, and gave the individual an air of purpose. It was only natural, then, that these entities be given at least some form of countenance so that humans could better communicate with them and perhaps understand their moods.

Thus, these vague and nebulous energies that populated the wilderness around the great settlements of the Middle East began to take on quasi-human characteristics. They became the *djinn* or *djinnii* of Middle Eastern folklore and legend. In the center of the swirling clouds of dust and air, there was a face that looked out on the world and that might speak to those who encountered it. It might utter prophecies or curses, sometimes in an arcane language. Those who communicated with the djinn were sometimes known as the *kahinn,* the oracle mongers, men who were sometimes driven mad by the knowledge the beings imparted to them. These were men who bridged the gap between the human and Natural worlds and might be privy to the secrets of the Universe. These were the men who sat in the corner of the market squares offering terrifying visions of the world around them to anyone who cared to listen.

The Djinn

The djinn or djinnii usually dwelt in caves or under the flat and sandy desert, but occasionally they were also creatures of the woods and forests. In some Islamic literature, we find references to an entity known as Al-Khidir—the "Green Thing." This being may have started as a vegetation god that was found in some of the forests, perhaps in northern Turkey. This may have once been an incredibly ancient god whose worship might have died out for a time but was then reenergized to flourish in the medieval Islamic world. Although references to it are sparse and scattered, there is no doubt that this deity was once widely worshipped, and was closely associated with trees and foliage. Could this perhaps be an early form of the Middle Eastern Green Man?

Al-Khidir

Al-Khidir, indeed, may be the mysterious spiritual "Companion" or guide to Moses that is mentioned in the Koran. Although there is much debate as to who the Companion actually *was* (some scholars say that he was the son of Imran, others argue that he was a completely different character), it is often accepted that it was actually the Biblical Patriarch. In this role, Al-Khidir was a direct channel to the Living God and advised Moses in many respects, taking on the role of counselor and, perhaps, Shaman. He was a repository of ancient wisdom, much of it concerning the Natural world—the so-called Secrets of the Universe. In fact, in some ancient mythologies, Al-Khidir was depicted as dwelling in the "Cave of Secrets" or the "Cave of Ancestral Wisdom" (the location of this site was never given and was allegedly only known to a very select few) out of which he pushed his head in order to be consulted. In this manner, he is also said to have acted as advisor to Alexander the Great during the 4th century B.C. He is said to have imbued great skills and success on the Macedonian conqueror, although Alexander himself is supposed to have attributed his military and political prowess to the Egyptian god Ammon. Yet, the idea of Al-Khidir as a wise face peering out of the darkness of a cave is a very striking and enduring one, and undoubtedly found its way into later Middle Eastern folklore.

In some parts of the Middle East, Al-Khidir's name is sometimes translated as "verdant," "fruitful," or "luxuriant," all phrases that might well be used to describe the Green Man and the ripening and reawakening of Nature. Connected with this description are legends (confusing, contradictory, and often portraying him as something akin to a human) concerning his descent into the Underworld in search of the "knowledge of the ancients" and his return to the surface world as a quasi-god. These tales may well have been influenced by the Greek legend of Orpheus who descends into Hades in search of his lover Eurydice, or several other similar legends from other cultures. One other interesting fact to note about Al-Khidir is that his color was green, which is suggestive of a Natural connection. He also appears to be connected to flowers and herbs, and prayers were sometimes offered to him when spices, ground from various herbs, were added to cooked dishes for seasoning or flavor.

It is also worthy of note that green is a "spiritual" color in Islam. The Islamic Paradise is believed to be lush, verdant, and green. Green is also the color of the 12th or "hidden" *imam* or spiritual leader who, it is prophesied, will reveal himself when the world is in great crisis. This savior is said to be living somewhere on a white island in the middle of a green ocean. The very appearance of this imam will cause a destroyed world to renew and revitalize itself. The echoes of the European Green Man here are obvious. The color green also represents knowledge and ancient wisdom, and those who are associated with it are considered to be especially wise and virtuous.

The Brazen Head

There is yet another aspect to the head of Al-Khidir peering from its Cave of Ancestral Wisdom. Earlier we noted how the Templars, returning from the Holy Land where they had taken part in the Crusades, brought back a "wondrous secret" with them. According to some traditions, this was a head made of brass. Some folklorists have named the head "Baphomet," although this may not have been strictly accurate because the name is suggestive of "Mohammed," representing the great Islamic prophet. Baphomet was more often used in the Christian West during the medieval period to refer to the Devil in his incarnation as the Goat of Mendes. It is possible that the name was simply trumped up by the Church during the trials of the Templar Order during the early-to-mid-1300s. It later enjoyed something of a resurgence during the late 1950s and early 1960s with the rise of Anton LaVey and the Church of Satan when it was falsely attributed to the occultist Eliphas Lévi. The Satanic Church adopted it as a symbol and placed it at the

center of a Satanic pentacle, thus firmly connecting it with diabo-
lism and evil. The Goat of Mendes is, of course, an incarnation of
the ram-headed god Ammon, who was worshipped in Mendes,
Egypt.

However, according to a widespread tradition, the brass head
was real enough, although exactly what its significance to the Order
might have been is not really known. The Templars were accused of
worshipping it or encouraging it to issue prophesies or pieces of
arcane wisdom. Worship of the Brazen Head was also supposed to
ensure fruitfulness and fertility on Templar lands. The figure later
became the mummified head of Jesus, taken from the tomb in the
rock by the Templars themselves, and was supposed to have the
power "to make the earth flower and the trees bear fruit." What
became of this Brazen Head after the dissolution of the Order is
unknown. It is thought that it was taken to a French village (the
Templars had originated amongst the French knights during the
Crusades) named Rennes-le-Chateau in the Languedoc (now
Languedoc-Roussillon). Other folklorists have stated that the already-
mentioned head of the Green Man in Rosslyn Chapel near
Edinburgh in Scotland is also based on the image of the Brazen
Head. In fact, some legends say that from the mouth of the artifact,
flowers and vegetation poured forth, very much in the style of the
Rosslyn carving. Whether or not the Head was ever held in Rosslyn
is a matter for conjecture. This was supposed to be the Head of Al-
Khidir, which had been found by the Templars in a secret room,
part of the Temple of Solomon from which they took their name.
Some authorities state that the Head is now hidden somewhere by
the Masonic Order, who are said to be the successors of the Knights
Templar; but no one is sure exactly where it might be located.

It remains one of the many enduring mysteries surrounding the Templars.

In the late 1880s and early 1890s, however, the village of Rennes-le-Chateau became the center of much speculation concerning the Order when the parish priest there, Berenger Sauniere, suddenly became inexplicably wealthy and was able to refurbish the church at his own expense; he also built a magnificent villa for himself. There were many theories as to how he had come by such good fortune—many of them connected to the Templars. Rumor was rife, for example, that he had found ancient parchments in the church, which revealed the location of a great treasure; others said that he had been paid a substantial sum by the Catholic Church not to reveal certain items he found there, perhaps thought to be the bones of Christ. Others still, however, claimed that he had found the Brazen Head of Al-Khidir, which had been hidden by the Templars in a hollow pillar within the church, and that this had brought him good fortune. Whatever the explanation, Sauniere never revealed the secret; if he *had* found the head, noone knows what became of it. The affairs at Rennes-le-Chateau became one of the great "Mysteries of the Templars," which recently received a new lease on life in Dan Brown's *The Da Vinci Code*.

Tibetan Buddhism

The Arabs and early Semites were not the only ancient peoples to embrace the idea of the Westernised Green Man, for the faces of ancient deities similar to Herne and Al-Khidir appear even further east. This may have been due to such beliefs traveling along the Spice Routes. Or perhaps they were indigenous entities that gradually emerged amongst the peoples of the East.

The idea of the verdant face also appears within the complex systems of beliefs that make up the Buddhist world. In Tibetan Buddhism, for example, the word for mask is *mukha,* which forms the basis for belief in an entity known as *Kirtimukha.* The name literally means "Face of Glory" and was used as a decorative icon in both Tibetan and Indian art. In Tibet, for instance, the face design is known as *makara vakstra* and appears as one of the central images on a cloth door-hanging called a *toran.* This is hung, complete with design, at the door of each dwelling to ensure both fertility and good luck for all those within. However, this is not a kind or gentle— even welcoming—countenance. It has protruding eyes and a gaping mouth with protruding canine teeth, which look ready to tear the watcher to shreds. On either side of the head, just above the temples, are two small and stubby horns, reminiscent of antlers. The whole aspect of the face is demonic, and one of ferocity. The reason for this is to frighten away evil forces that might threaten the home. In some representations of the Kirtimukha, the open mouth trails vines and creepers, which spill out as if to grasp the onlooker in a deadly embrace, pulling him or her in towards the razor fangs. Kirtimukha is something of an ambivalent entity in Tibetan folklore. He is certainly a deity who brings good fortune and relative prosperity to those who serve and respect him, but he can also be a destroyer and a devastator, bringing heavy rains, which can utterly ruin the crops that he creates. He is also the guardian of very ancient knowledge that he will release to his followers in a sparing manner and only when asked directly through the medium of a lama (or Shaman). Some of these notions can also be attributed to the Green Man.

Indra

The face could be that of an ancient Tibetan vegetation god or Nature spirit—probably of great antiquity—and yet similar images appear all through the north of India and sometimes further afield. Throughout northern India, the cult of Indra once held sway. Indra was a corn god who was in charge of the ripening crop, ensuring that new shoots rose "from the husks of the old." He was the god who brought the rain and renewed and revived the thirsty earth after the hot summer days. Originally, Indra may have been a water god but he later became associated in the Indian mind with growth and vegetation. In some of his aspects, Indra is rather similar to Kirtimukha. He is a capricious and ambivalent entity that can destroy as well as create, and he is also a repository of ancient wisdom. In later times, he became the equivalent of a storm god, riding across the heavens, following the sun in a chase, which resembles the Wild Hunt of Celtic folklore. In fact, Indra's chase across the sky usually signals the approach of storms and wind turbulence, just as the Wild Hunt did in Britain. Indra is also portrayed as a mighty and fearless warrior, who continually drives his war-chariot across the sky, thus placing him in the same league as the old warrior kings of Celtic mythology who seemed to be caught up in the Wild Hunt itself. Such a connection often displays some of the close links between Eastern and European mythologies and the influence that one has managed to exert upon the other.

Vishnu

The Eastern Hindu divinity that is most closely associated with Indra is Vishnu. The name means "The Preserver," but etymologists argue that it may come from a much older Indo-European source meaning "unlimited" or "without restrictions" (literally "without fetters"), and may refer to an all-pervasive force that was worshipped in very early times. The name can also be translated as "turning his face to all sides," which seems to strengthen the suggestion of no restrictions; the implication is that this was originally the all-pervasive force of Nature. He is often seen as both creator and destroyer—first destroying living things and then creating new life from them in the cycle of death and rebirth. In early mythology, Vishnu was said to have taken "three great steps" across the Earth and where he put his feet, vegetation sprouted forth, linking him inevitably with growth and luxuriance. This, of course, contains echoes of the Western Green Man, who appears to have traveled eastward.

Although neither Indra nor Vishnu are simply faces in the style of Kirtimukha—"the Face of Glory"—they certainly do represent some aspects of the Green Man as he appears in the West, and they do appear centrally and extensively in Indian art. Both are regarded as a symbol of luck when placed on cloths and coverings. Perhaps this is connected to the fertility and fecundity associated with them in their earlier incarnations.

Tammuz

Another rather interesting deity that is worshipped in parts of southern India is Tammuz. Tammuz or Tammuzh appears in the mythologies and ancient literature of both southern India and Sri Lanka (Ceylon). He also appears in the early Sumerian accounts from the Middle East. This connection may have come about through the Spice Trade or early links between Southern India/ Ceylon and Egypt, or through Phoenician traders from Lebanon.

His name was prominent in Babylonian worship where he is often depicted in early representations as a kind of shepherd-god in charge of Nature. Indeed, it has been argued that the name Tammuz (thought to have been adapted from the name of an older Akkadian deity Dumuzid or Dumuzi) may have meant "lord" (as of Nature) and might have formed the basis for the name of the Syrian/Greek god Adonis.

Originally, it was thought Tammuz was a fisher-king who emerged from the waters that covered Earth to bring fertility and plenty to the land. So closely was Tammuz associated with growth and fertility that, as the days grew shorter and the light began to decline, the Babylonians assumed that the god was dead and had descended into the Underworld; a mock "funeral" was held for him all across Babylonia and the eastern Aegean. These may well have had similar traditional roots to the dances and festivities that were held to mark the death of the King of the Wood in Celtic lands. The "funerals" for Tammuz became so widespread that they were even performed at the gates of the Temple in Jerusalem itself, invoking the anger of the prophet and reformer Ezekiel:

> Then he brought me to the door of the gate of the LORD's house which was toward the north, and behold, there sat women, weeping for Tammuz. And he said to me "Hast thou seen this, O Son of Man? Turn thou yet again and thou shalt see abominations greater than these" (Ezekiel 8: 14–15).

The righteous indignity of the prophet serves to underscore the widespread acceptance of the Tammuz cult throughout the Middle East.

He is also mentioned further east, in the Sangam texts where he is described as a king of Kur. Although Sanskrit is a religious language of the East, Sangam is a much more secular form, detailing the exploits of warriors, political systems, and so forth. Tammuz is described in the Sangam texts as being one of the Pandyan kings ruling over an ancient realm that was the forerunner of the Tamil people. In Babylonian mythology Tammuz is also described as a ruler of ancient Uruk, a city within the Sumerian Empire. This lay to the south of Babylon and has been identified by some historians and archaeologists as the possible site of Ur of the Chaldees, from which the Biblical Patriarchs—in particular Abraham—came. If this is true, then it was an area steeped in mysticism and so-called hidden knowledge. Ur of the Chaldees was also, in some legends, the place where ancient sorcerers controlled the djinni and created powerful magics. Chaldean sorcerers also acted as advisors to some of the ancient Middle Eastern kings.

In both Sumerian and Tamil legend, the story of Tammuz and/or Dumuzi is roughly the same. In the original Sumerian fable and in the Sumerian Table of Kings, Tammuz or Dumuzi is confusingly given as the king of Kua or Kuadam, an ancient city that was overwhelmed by a massive flood around 1750 B.C.—a date that incidentally corresponds with accounts of the Flood mentioned in the Book of Genesis. Even more confusingly, a king named Dumu-zid appears as ruler of a city named Endu (near the city of Ur or Uruku) *after* the Flood (the Sumerian Table of Kings cites him as the fifth king following the Great Deluge). It is said that he reigned for more than 100 years, but lived much longer and was "god-like" in his ways. Starting out as a fisher-king, Dumuzi seems to have quickly become a shepherd figure, appearing as such in early Babylonian art, though when the change came about is not certain. As such, he seems to have been in control of both animals and vegetation in the early Babylonian world.

In the Sumerian texts Tammuz/Dumuzi seized the throne, which had been vacated by Queen Immana who had gone to the Underworld to be judged by the Anunnaki, a panel of 50 minor gods. There she was found guilty of misusing her great powers over Nature and was condemned to death. Nevertheless, her faithful servant pleaded with the major gods of the Sumerian pantheon to restore her to life, but only one responded. This was Enki, the "Lord of the Waters Under the Earth" who was regarded in Sumerian mythology as something of a trickster. He placed several conditions on the restoration of Immana, although what these conditions were varies from one tale to another. Whatever the conditions were, they appear to have been met; Immana was restored to life and set out from the Underworld to reclaim her throne. According to the early Akkadian texts, the final condition of her return to life was to search for a replacement for herself in the Nether Regions and to encourage him or her to go there (that is, to die ritually). Returning to her kingdom, she found Tammuz/Dumuzi on the throne (in some versions of the tale he is her husband)—he had not been displeased that she was gone, and had taken over the realm as his own. Angered, Immana declared that he would be her replacement in the Underworld and called upon demons to convey him thither.

It is here that the Akkadian texts break down into a number of conflicting and fragmentary tales. One of these concerns Tammuz's sister Beli, who announces that Tammuz will return from the dead and will rule again. Other fragmentary tales refer to a prophesy by the hag Geshtinana—also said to be Tammuz's sister—saying roughly the same thing. It is not clear, however, whether Tammuz was torn to pieces by the demons that Immana had summoned, but it is clear that he came back from the dead, as the tale of his return from the Underworld appears in all the folkloric fragments. However, there were complications with his revival. He found himself hunted by demons intent on taking him back with them to the Underworld and he was forced to hide. Eventually Immana relented and a deal was struck. Tammuz/Dumuzi would spend only six months in the Realm of the Dead and upon his return to the surface world, his place would be taken by his sister Beli (or by Gashtinana). When he left the world of the living, the world would become bleak and cold and many growing things would die. Later, in light of this belief, Tammuz himself actually became a god of vegetation and growth.

This legend was an explanation for the seasons and for the harvest (everything had to be gathered in before Tammuz left the world or else it would die). It also serves as an explanation for the elaborate "funerals" for the god, against which the prophet Ezekiel raged.

The legend seems to have transferred to the ancient Tamil culture of Sri Lanka (Ceylon) and Southern India, where similar tale exists through the latter's contact with Ptolemaic Egypt and through trade with what is now the Middle East. In Tamil mythology he is known as Tammuzh or Pandion, a Pandyan king who had his capital in Kuadam (otherwise known as Kapadapuram), supposedly in the south of India. In a variant of the legend, he managed to escape from the Underworld but was pursued by fiends who literally tore him to pieces. All that survived of him was his head, which was the seat (or essence) of his being, and enabled him to restore at leas part of his physical body. The other section was carried off back to the Underworld, which meant that to be reunited, Tammuz had to travel there for a number of months in the year, during which time vegetation died and there were no crops

A ghastly pall—the pall of winter—also hung over the city of Kuadam, which was in mourning for its ruler. In his human incarnation, Tammuz is described as being one of the kings of the Chola Dynasty, mentioned in Sangam literature; they were believed to have ruled in southern India from around C.E. 898 to 1279. This dynasty is divided into three distinct sections—Early, Medieval, and Chalukya eras—and it is thought that Tammuzh belonged to the earliest of those. He is probably one of a number of legendary Sumerian figures—god-hero-kings—who were later transformed into gods, venerated by subsequent generations. There are many parallels in his story to the early Egyptian legends of Osiris/Isis, and it may be that one mythology influenced the other. Of course, the universal ideas of death and resurrection that are used to explain the waxing and waning of the seasons appear in many ancient mythologies—for example, Greek and Celtic—but here they have a special resonance.

The Tamil legend of the head of Tammuzh surviving after his body was ripped to pieces by demons following his escape from the Underworld, also contains resonances of the Celtic Green Man. This connection is strengthened by the idea in the fable that the head appears to have power over Nature and over creation, and Nature is therefore able to at least partially restore Tammuzh's body. This power makes Tammuzh a god of creation, growth, and vegetation, and gives him an intensely close connection with the Natural world.

The Far East

Faces and Heads

Faces and heads were also important in Far Eastern culture and superstition; here too they seem to be associated with plenty and good fortune. In certain rural provinces in northern China, for example, it is customary to paint faces on the sides of water gourds and storage jars in order to ensure plentifulness and abundance for the household. Curiously, the more disfigured and grotesque the face, the more luck proceeds into the household around it. Thus, painters illustrate these jars and gourds with choleric or "measled" (measles is still a fatal disease in some parts of China) countenances that may be truly horrific. In some cases, fire, water, or foliage flows from their mouths and sometimes even encircles the container in its embrace. According to tradition, these are supposed to be the representations of minor demons or localized fertility gods who oversee the crops and livestock of the various districts. It has also been argued that these are localized variants of the Tibetan Kirtimukha— "the Face of Glory"—referred to earlier.

Another variation of the Kirtimukha could be found in the Apo Kayam region of Borneo where it was also a symbol of good luck and plenty. This is the image of a head or face, often sprouting vegetation and foliage from its mouth, which is woven into cloths and even into baskets that are laid around the house to bring good fortune and full bellies to all around. The face is even woven into the baskets on which local women carry their babies as a symbol of well-being throughout the infants' lives. In this region Kirtimukha is regarded as a god of vegetation and ripening corn, and is therefore associated with food and social stability.

The Lord Rishabha

The same face that appears in Borneo also appears in parts of India where it is revered by the Jains and, in fact, is carved into the decoration of some of their temples. In the celebrated marble temple at Ranakpur (Ranakpuhr) in Rajasthan, western India, for instance, several Green Man-like heads can be seen peering out from amongst the leaves of the decorative carvings. These may reflect a much older former temple dedicated to Adinath (Adinatha), the Lord Rishabha. This deity was widely regarded as the Lord of Light and also a god of fertility and growth (which was associated with light and warmth). He taught the people about agriculture and the care of animals. However, there was a darker side to the Lord Rishabha as well, for he could also bring rains and winds that could instantly destroy the crops and create famine, plague, and sickness in their wake. The small heads hidden amongst the foliage were said to be minor gods or demons that carried out his will amongst Men. Perhaps they are representations of some ancient pre-Jain forest deities.

Colors also have a special significance in Eastern cosmology. The celestial color blue—used to signify life and power—is often used to symbolize the gods of the Hindu worlds, for example. However, it must also be remembered that the colors blue and green are often interchangeable in this respect, and thus while Krishna, the eighth avatar of Vishnu, nicknamed "the Preserver," is usually depicted as having blue skin, it may be possible to argue that he is based on an older entity that was green skinned and was firmly connected to the Natural world.

Duk-Duk

The South Pacific

The Duk-Duk

The idea of faces peering from the forest to terrorize people can also be found in some South Pacific cultures, as can the belief in a being dwelling deep amongst the trees and having control over Nature. Amongst the Austrolasian peoples of eastern New Britain, a province of Papua New Guinea, there is a widespread belief in the Duk-Duk, the wild man of the forests. Indeed, so widespread was this belief in former times that a secret society containing both religious and political influences was formed to carry out his will throughout the provincial communities. The Duk-Duk was an alarming figure. It was the epitome of wildness—a gigantic creature, trailing vines and creepers in its wake, wearing a skirt made of leaves, and a huge, conical helmet made of cane and wicker. But the most frightening thing about the Duk-Duk was its face—huge and wrapped about with the foliage of the forest, with a grinning or yawning mouth, and wide, circular, staring eyes. (In some eastern New Britain societies, the Duk-Duk was faceless and the foregoing description applied to a variant of the entity known as the *tuban*.) Women and children were forbidden to look upon this dreadful countenance and would be struck dead if they attempted to do so. The Duk-Duk only appeared in person at night and only when there was a full moon. He emerged from the forest to issue his commands, which had to be strictly obeyed or else the forces of Nature would be turned against those who refused or ignored the instructions. However, during the daytime he allegedly watched from the forest—in the style of a peering and wary face—for those who worked against him or who were lax in performing their duties. He was also regarded as a kind of protector of the forest, albeit a somewhat tyrannical and hostile one.

Unlike some other Green Man-type figures, the Duk-Duk had a profound influence on both local and regional politics in the area of New Britain. As King of the Forest, his word was law amongst local politicians and he even had a number of men who went about, dressed similar to himself, wearing frightening masks and stylized ceremonial heads, to enforce his wishes. These men behaved as though they were secret police, carrying out summary justice, enforcing special taxes and levies set by the Duk-Duk, and generally "taking care" of those who spoke out against the Lord of the Forest. In this they behaved pretty much in the style of the *Ton-Ton Macoute* in Haiti during the Duvalier regime. All of them wore special tuban masks, which were supposed to confer supernatural powers upon the wearer. The Duk-Duk therefore became something of a political tyrant amongst the islanders of New Britain, and his authority was enforced through representations of his foliage-swathed face. Of late, however, his power in the rural regions has greatly decreased and, although his secret society is still said to survive in certain areas, his followers no longer enjoy the power they once had. The face of the Duk-Duk or the tuban have now become quaint pieces of New Guinea folk art and the cancers that once accompanied him on his appearances have become little more than a tourist attraction.

Mesoamerica

Although this section has primarily focused attention on the fertility and vegetation gods of the East, it may also be apposite to look

briefly at some of the gods of early pre-Columban America—
the period that historians and archaeologists often refer to as
Mesoamerica.

Chicomecoatl

In this period, the gods worshipped by the various inhabitants
of the early American continent were often violent and bloody.
However, some of them had their benign side as well. The early
peoples, such as the Toltecs who were dwelling in Mexico in the 9th
and 10th centuries, depended largely on maize as a source of sustenance. Their corn goddess (and the goddess of growing things) was
Chicomecoatl, deity of fertility and maize. She would later go on to
hold a similar position amongst other ancient peoples, such as the
Aztecs, whose rulers claimed direct descendancy from the Toltec
peoples. There is a distinct possibility that, as a fertility goddess,
Chicomecoatl preceded even the Toltecs, and she is described as "a
very ancient god." Widely regarded as the goddess of foodstuffs
and vegetation, her name means "Seven Serpents" and she was the
centre of a maize cult, which venerated both her and the growing
corn. A great feast was held in her honor during the month of Huei
Tozoztli (April–May) the name meaning "prolonged fast." After this
month was past, however, there was much eating, drinking, and
dancing in the manner of some of the May revels in early modern
England and elsewhere. Representations of the goddess were carved
on water bottles and pots, and always (as in ancient China) in the
form of a head. The carving was intended to signify good luck and
plenty.

Just to confuse matters even further, Chicomecoatl was not
always a woman. It is thought that amongst earlier civilizations

than the Toltecs, she appeared as Centeotl, a male corn god—again depicted mainly through the medium of a face either carved in pottery or painted on the sides of jars. Just when the transformation across the genders took place is largely unknown, but it is thought to have been amongst the early Toltecs or their forerunners.

Tlaloc

Chicomecoatl did not rule the world of vegetation and growth alone, however. Her companion was Tlaloc, a deity that also seems to have been accepted by the Aztecs from an earlier culture, and who was the god of water and rain. In some traditions, he is described as being an early ruler of the city of Chichén Itzá, which was once the center and principal settlement of the Yucatán peninsula in Mexico. Tlaloc was a ferocious god, demanding human sacrifice, usually of children (who were ritually drowned in his honor), whose tears were actually the entity's sustenance.

Tlaloc was usually depicted as a great face with two small prehensile hands on either side. In the mythology of El Salvador, he is simply shown as a great face usually with fangs and snorting nostrils, trailing either smoke or vegetation. He was an ambivalent entity, bringing the rains that allowed the maize to grow and ripen, but also bringing destructive thunderstorms and flash floods. In Aztec mythology, he was also married to Xochiquetzal (his first wife), a goddess of flowers, herbs, and other growing things, and who was sometimes portrayed as a great face. Although originally thought to have been a Toltec (or perhaps even older) god, Tlaloc was quickly accepted by the Aztecs, who sometimes wove his face into their baskets and used it as the basis for some pottery ornamentation. The entity was taken up by the Maya who also inhabited Yucatán and worshipped Tlaloc as their own god Chac (or Chaac). Chac had many similar attributes but was mostly a god of maize and fertility.

Xilonan

Another female Aztec deity who often appeared as a face was Xilonan, another corn goddess. Confusingly, she may also be a later incarnation of Chicomecoatl, as many of the earlier gods received new names under incoming invaders. Xilonan—the "goddess of young corn"—was often perceived as a great head, hung about with shaggy tassels to suggest the unshucked corn. She appeared in mythology as the wife of the Aztec god Tezcatlipoca, Lord of the Smoking Mirror and god of night and darkness, who was something of a trickster and was widely regarded as an enemy of Mankind. As such, Xilonan was an extremely powerful goddess and in some aspects at least, was not considered well-disposed towards humans. A number of ritualized human sacrifices were carried out each year in order to placate her.

Xipe Totec

The last of the major Mesoamerican deities to be represented by a great face was Xipe Totec or "Xipe the Flayed One," a fertility god of the coastal Zepotec and Yopi cultures in Yucatán, Mexico. This face was rather unique and startling in the realm of Green Men/fertility gods, as the image of a flayed human skull represented the god in some forms of Aztec art. At other times, he is simply portrayed as a slightly distorted terra-cotta head—a number of which appear to have been created between 900 and 1521. He is also portrayed as a deformed-looking dwarf or as a beautiful golden man.

Amongst the Aztecs, however, Xipe Totec was considered to be a "foreign god" and his temples bore the name Yopico ("the Yopi place"). A general worship of Xipe amongst the Aztecs seems to have commenced during the reign of the Emperor Axayacatl (1469–1481).

Xipe was also regarded as the Lord of Spring (the coming of the rainy season when vegetation grew), disappearing into and reemerging from the Underworld in a belief reminiscent of the life-death-rebirth cycles that we discussed earlier. Each year he ritually flayed himself, the shedding skin representing the husks of the maize, which gave sustenance to his followers. Xipe was a highly ambivalent god—he fed and sustained his people while at the same time bringing disease, plague, and sickness amongst them. Part of his worship also involved the ritual skinning of specially chosen followers, and his priests often wore robes made from flayed human skin. He was also a god of agriculture and fertility in women. Yet, even this had its rather gruesome side. It is believed that a ritual sacrifice was carried out and the thighbone taken from the corpse. This was dedicated to Xipe—the god was believed to inhabit it—and those wishing to be with child were ceremonially touched by the bone in the hands of a priest. Those who were so touched were said to fall pregnant within the year. Thus in ritual death, new life was created. This notion, of course, contained recognizable echoes of the Green Man in Western Europe.

Huitzilopochtli

A number of both minor and major Aztec gods and goddesses are also peripherally associated with fertility and regeneration in the style of the Green Man. One of these is Huitzilopochtli, a Nahua god of war who was also adopted by the Aztecs, though when this took place is not completely clear. Although a god of battle and destruction, Huitzilopochtli was also associated with agriculture and the ripening maize; it is possible that he may have had some of the elements of another, more agriculturally based deity, incorporated into him. Of special interest, one of the representations of the deity was that of a blackened face. His worship amongst the Aztecs was encouraged by the noble Tlacaelel (1397–1487), brother of Moctezuma I, although the vegetational and fertility aspects of his person were not particularly emphasised, and he was portrayed more as a warrior god—the sacred hummingbird. (It was believed in the middle and later Aztec periods that the souls of famous or powerful warriors often returned from the Underworld in the guise of butterflies or hummingbirds.) Under the Aztecs, his associations with vegetation and Nature became more and more tenuous.

A number of other such peripheral deities also feature in Mesoamerican mythology, but few have the direct connections to the Natural world that are evidenced by the European aspects of the Green Man. And yet the ideas of an ambivalent Nature and of life, death, and rebirth are often reflected in even early American indigenous cultures.

African Nature Entities

On the African continent too, we can often find some of the same beliefs and concerns. Unlike the civilizations of the Middle East and the early Mesoamerican cultures, such beliefs tend to be slightly less coherent, belonging not to a readily identifiable pantheon, but to loose confederations of spirits and forces that inhabit the African jungles and forests. These entities serve largely as protectors and defenders of Nature, but they also may ensure good hunting and the well-being of various communities scattered across rural regions. They can also be capricious and even belligerent to those who cross them or to whom they take a dislike. They are exceptionally powerful, able to level entire communities with a windstorm or a flood, and are fiercely territorial, being seen as lords of certain districts or woodlands. Many of them are simply disembodied forces, which nevertheless maintain a watching and wary stance with regard to humans. Some of these beings, however, appear as carvings of faces and heads, almost in the style of the Green Man, which are venerated amongst certain African peoples. For many African tribes—similar to the early English—the head was the center of power in the body and the face was what gave the individual his or her identity—so a richly decorated carven head or face manifested authority and influence.

The Simbi

Amongst such Nature entities—and closely connected with trees—are the *simbi* who appear both in Central and West Africa, and who are sometimes represented by carvings and masks. Some of the carvings are portrayed on the trunks of trees, around which a shrine has been made and offerings are left. It is not clear, however, whether the word *simbi* is a collective one, referring to a number of spirits, or whether it refers to one single entity. The simbi is or are very old, having existed since the dawn of time when the forests were very young. Although belief in it or them is now dying out, traditions still remain strong in parts of West Africa. Simbi are sometimes represented by an old and wrinkled face, which has been carved into masks or ornamented heads (of both clay and wood), which are then worn by their devotees. Some of these are elaborately decorated, but others are simply left plain—emphasising both age and wisdom, as well as the Natural world.

In past times, the simbi (as extremely powerful entities) took an active part of local and regional politics. As with the Duk-Duk in eastern New Britain, their word was law, and if not obeyed it was believed that they would unleash a terrible vengeance upon the community. The masks themselves (even when not worn by their adherents) were supposed to exert supernatural influences; simply to touch them could bring about healing and possible good fortune.

The simbi were extremely capricious, even childlike in their ways, so frequent and elaborate attempts to appease them (or it) were carried out. While they were closely associated with vegetation, they also sent droughts and spread disease. As well as being wrinkled faces, they took on the guise of birds and flies, but it was the lined and adorned countenance, perhaps carved on a tree or resembling a head in some woodland shrine, which was really the focus of worship. It was said that such images had the power of speech, and it was to Shamans and/or local politicians that the simbi could make their (or its) wishes known.

It is also interesting to note that although the simbi are considered to be largely an African phenomenon, the name also appears in the South Carolina Low Country of the United States of America. The reason for this probably lies in the importation of slaves from West Africa to work in the rice plantations scattered all through the south of the state. During the "reign" of the Rice Kings in South Carolina during the mid-19th century it was thought that thousands of slaves were worshipping tree beings. Consequently, the simbi became strongly connected with the cult of *voudou* (voodoo) and the Nature deities (deity) latterly became *loa* or a spirit in the voodoo pantheon. In the 1840s, a wave of worship by slaves wearing masks and worshipping heads occurred on several of the major South Carolina plantations, alarming some caucasians. However, during that year, the religious enthusiasm seemed to die away just as quickly as it had arisen. However, in certain parts of the Low Country, there are still whispers of spirit veneration at certain trees, which have been specially carved with faces, tucked away in remote locations.

For other ancient African peoples, trees, embodying the spirits of the woodland and the forces of Nature, also featured strongly. The ancient Akan people of Ghana for example, venerated and carved the Onyamodua tree (*alstonia boonei*), which they regarded as the center of their world and the shaper of their identity. Legends concerning the spirit of the tree are found in oral collections of their stories, known as *anansasam* (literally "spider stones" but a name for a wider group of oral tales) that it is said, have been passed down by word of mouth from earliest times. In these, it is claimed that the Onynamodua is the "Father of Trees," and it is somehow connected with the very fate of the world itself. It is possible that the spirit said to inhabit these trees is symbolic of a very ancient vegetation god that was worshipped by the early Akan people. The "Father of Trees" is thought to have been represented by a face woven onto sheets and blankets by the Akans.

Huntin

Other similar vegetation and Nature gods abound all across Africa. Toward the Cape for example, Huntin (or Huntan) is a tree god who is still venerated amongst the Xhosa peoples (a branch of the Bantu), found in the southeast of South Africa. Many of the Xhosa beliefs follow those of the ancient Akan people, believing that Huntin is the central god of the world and everything revolves around his sacred trees. He will also ensure good hunting and plentiful crops, as well as fertility amongst the Xhosa women, ensuring that the people remain strong and vibrant within themselves. His power over the Natural world is limitless. Sometimes, he is represented by a rather grotesque face made out of wood or wicker, which is the visible sign of his presence, and this perhaps is a key to the worship of the god amongst the rural African cultures. A recognizable face constitutes the visible and immediate presence of an otherwise disembodied entity—it is one that can be worshipped, venerated, and appeased in a logical, physical way. In many ways, indeed, the worship of such an image—that of a Nature or vegetation god—is a concrete, psychological example of reunification between Mankind and the Natural world that is all around. This again contains echoes of medieval/early modern England and its response to the face and figure of the Green Man.

All across the world and across the centuries, then, various cultures have sought to reestablish themselves with the Natural world in roughly similar ways, sometimes using roughly similar imagery and iconography. Underlying it all is the sense of *separateness* and sometimes threat, which we referred to earlier. In all of this, the Green Man, or some similar entity, has served as a physical focus for such a yearning. Whether it is in the East or the West, both the human rationale and the impetus are still the same.

Chapter

Unholy Terrors

Arguably no formally recognized religion fit in so well with the Green Man, as did Christianity. Although it may well appear as a blasphemy to the strictly pious, the imagery of the Christian message might well have been borrowed from the Pagan perception. Consider the scenario—the King of the Wood (the representation of the god) is ritually killed for his people and rises once again, restored to save his people and bring about their well-being. During the ritual sacrifice, blood is ceremonially spilled. The sacrifice restores the god's favor and the King is placed onto a higher, almost godlike plane. All is well with the world as a result of the sacrifice, and the King's followers enjoy well-being and reign with him over Nature. Compare this with the basic Christian message. Jesus Christ dies on the Cross as a willing sacrifice for his people (to atone for their sins). Three days later He is resurrected and ascends to reign over the world at the

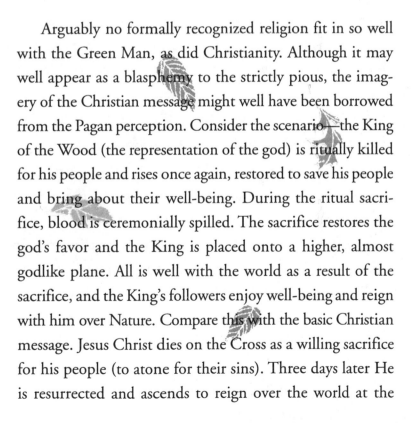

Right Hand of God. Through his sacrifice, the sinful world is cleansed and made right. Those who followed Christ are "rulers with Him in Glory." They are guaranteed a kind of wonderful Paradise, which has earthly overtones—glorious meadows, eternal sunshine, sparkling streams, and the sweetly scented waft of beautiful flowers. There is also a further belief that Christ will return as King to usher in a new era of peace, harmony, and contentment. The two scenarios are almost identical, both in nature and tone. Even the imagery that permeates the Christian belief is striking similar—"washed in the Blood"; "the Lamb of God" (suggesting ritual Middle Eastern sacrifice young lambs or sheep were often used); "the Good Shepherd." All these are suggestive of earlier Pagan ritual and ideology, and it is possible that at least some of the early Christian perspective emerged out of the Middle Eastern resurrection cults (for example, those of Osiris and the yearly "resurrection" of the man-god Mithras).

In its earliest inception, of course, Christianity seems to have "borrowed" some elements from other Middle Eastern cults—for example, the Virgin Birth and the coming of the Magi from the cult of Mithras—and it was largely left to the apostle Paul to weld this early mishmash of beliefs and ideas into a coherent, recognizable, and distinctive dogma. The notions of innocent sacrifice and resurrection, however, were still central to the emerging faith. Indeed, the concepts of renewal and rebirth were (and still are) at the core of the Christian faith. Today, some Christian groups talk about believers being "born again," being "reborn in Christ," or being "cleansed anew in Christ's blood," and although this is generally believed to be a spiritual (not a physical) rebirth, the concept of renewal and cleansing are still clearly evident within this highly symbolic language.

Although a more developed Christianity railed against Pagan practices, Pagan idols, and even Pagan imagery, it was not slow to incorporate them into its own religious structure in order to attract and gain new converts. Old Pagan shrines simply were transferred to Christian saints and the former Pagan powers that were often associated with them (such as healing) were now simply ascribed to the power of God. The idea of a man-god dying, descending into the Underworld, and then rising again from the tomb, fit in well with many of the beliefs held by the surrounding Pagan peoples, and no doubt may have aided Christianity's spread.

The Christian Theme of Resurrection and Renewal

It was in Western Europe that a unified orthodox Christianity really took hold. While the Middle East and Eastern Europe squabbled over theological differences and finally fractured and split, much of the West centered around a fairly rigid dogma, which focused on the resurrection and renewal offered by Christ. One of the reasons for this may have been due to the powerful goddesses of renewal and rebirth in both Anglo-Saxon and Germanic cultures.

Eostre

One of the major deities in large parts of the West (including Britain) was the Anglo-Saxon goddess Eostre. She has become largely associated with England because one of the few accounts concerning her comes from an English churchman—the Venerable Bede (672–735) in his writing *De Tempore Ratione* (*On the Reckoning of*

Time), who describes the month of April (Eostrremanant in the Germanic calendar) as being her month. Eostre was the Anglo-Saxon goddess of spring and a rough translation of her name is usually given as "dawn" or "daybreak." However, it is also possible that it may mean "renewal" or "reinvigoration," and may refer to a vegetation deity. Her symbols were supposedly those of a hare (or rabbit) and an egg, although it is not clear if these were in fact her symbols. It is possible that these refer to another Germanic vegetation goddess named Ostern or Ostera, and were mistakenly attributed to Eostre by the German folklorist and storyteller Jakob Grimm (1785–1863). Bede makes no mention of a major festival linked to Eostre, nor to any real symbols, but it is possible that a number of minor fertility and vegetation festivals concerning the spring and the return of growth were carried on during her month. Eostre was certainly a goddess connected with growth and greenery, as tradition tells us that she was connected with the opening of flowers, the rising of the sap, and the unfurling of leaves (hence the translation of her name as "dawn").

It seems appropriate that the Christian Church should have taken over her name for the celebration of Christ's death, His subsequent rising from the tomb (victory over Death and the Underworld), and His "renewal" as King—amending it to Easter, the major festival in the Christian calendar. However, possibly because there was no fixed feast for the goddess, no one seemed to agree on the exact date of this particular festival. The Celtic Church of the West (which was based on the island of Iona and exerted influence on Ireland, Scotland, Wales, and Cornwall, as well as parts of Britain and Gaul) observed one particular period, while the Roman Church followed another. A particular problem was that the period observed by the

Celtic Church followed the various phases of the moon (Eostre was also a moon goddess), and this practice could be regarded as Pagan by more dogmatic Christians. This allowed the Roman Church to describe its Celtic counterpart simply as "Pagans by another name." The great Synod of Whitby (A.D. 664) was specifically convened to resolve the exact date of Easter. This it failed to do, although it resolved a number of other issues in the Roman Church's favor, and today Easter in Western Europe still remains a "movable feast" tied to the waxing and waning of the moon. Thus, one of the most important Christian festivals, celebrating the central themes of the Christian religion—the death and resurrection of Christ and His cleansing of the world—is largely determined by a Pagan goddess of vegetation and fertility, a kind of feminine Green Man.

Christianity and Pagan Iconography

If Christians could incorporate Pagan goddesses into their formal religious structures, they could also do so with both Pagan ideology and iconography. We have already noted how the image of the Green Man was incorporated into the stonework at Rosslyn Chapel in Scotland, and how it was one of the Templar mysteries. It was not, however, the only instance of such iconography.

In early Christian Western Europe, there were numerous examples of ancient Pagan sites that had been taken over by Christians as their own. In Ireland and Scotland, for example, a great number of healing wells had been dedicated to certain saints, and their cures attributed to the powers of holy men rather than to some local spirit. On the former sites of Pagan worship too, churches had been erected and there was a widespread belief amongst Christians that the holy powers of a Godly place would take away the sinister Pagan influences and cleans the ground. It was also believed that Pagan stones or imagery, brought into sacred precincts, would lose their unholy powers when placed before God. However, there was also another, more subtle reason for the inclusion of Pagan relics and Pagan imagery in some places of worship.

In some parts of the West, Christianity took root slowly. It should not be assumed that Pagans immediately saw the wisdom and theological validity of the new religion and went to bed as Pagans only to wake up in the morning as Christians. Nor should it be thought that the former Pagan peoples unquestioningly accepted every aspect of the new religion. Many simply paid lip service to Christianity while retaining fundamental elements of their former faiths. There was also a widespread belief that the old gods were as powerful as they had always been but that their influence had simply been subsumed by the all-embracing Christian religion. And if it meant new "converts," many Church leaders were quite willing to go along with that view. It was thought, for example, that demons within a church might serve as a protection against the evil forces that sought entry there. This notion of old gods and their power continued down through the centuries, even after Christianity had been well-established in places such as Britain.

The Norman Period

In Britain there is no evidence of Green Man carving and ornamentation before the Morman period (in other words, before 1066). The earliest carvings of him are etched in stone in some of the early Norman cathedrals, monasteries, and churches, although these later gave way to wooden images. Such ornamentation and carving continued down through the medieval period, but suffered something of a decline with the rise of Protestantism. Such decoration later enjoyed a new phase during Victorian times with the rise of Gothic carving and restoration.

The inclusion of the Green Man in early Norman architecture may rise out of the Normans' interest in the notion of "greenness." For them it suggested otherworldly, though earthy, considerations. Fairies, when they were described, were stated as being "green" either in skin tone or in dress; certain Witches were described as "having green faces" and a number of fabulous monsters were denoted as being "green in hue." Green was the color of the forests, and it was also the color of concealment in an era when the green forests and woodlands covered greater parts of the country than they do today. Therefore, many of these entities traveled unseen by blending in with the Natural background. Green was also, in the Norman mind, a color that was closely associated with the supernatural or the unusual.

The Green Children

Some of their tales reflect this—for example the Green Children in the story recounted in Latin by Ralph of Coggeshall. In this narrative, the Cistercian abbot of Coggeshall Abbey in Essex tells of two green-skinned children, a boy and a girl, who were found by huntsmen near St. Mary's-by-the-Wolfpits (now Woolpit) and taken to the castle of a local Norman baron whose name is usually given as Sir Richard de Colne. There, they were treated as "wonders" and given the special protection of the Norman lord himself. They claimed to have come from a mysterious Underworld, having strayed

The Green Children

into our world by accident. They had come through some sort of mineshaft, which had been closed, and they found themselves unable to return to their former home. They were subsequently brought up on Sir Richard's estates and under his protection. The boy did not fare well on the surface world and became languid, pining for his home; eventually he died. The girl, however, lived on and, according to the abbot, became incredibly promiscuous, taking lovers everywhere. Finally, she ran off with a manservant and continued to live near King's Lynn for a number of years. However, on occasion she would return to St. Mary's-by-the-Wolfpits and look longingly around the area, as if seeking a shaft back to her Underworld home. One day, she simply vanished. These events occurred, according to Ralph, during the reign of King Stephen (1135–1154).

The tale of the Green Children circulated all through Norman England. The land from which they came was described as lying far beneath our feet and was supposedly quite similar to the medieval world on the surface, but more lush and covered in green vegetation. Although some attempts were made to find an entrance to it, none were successful.

The idea of green people and a lush, verdant Underworld seems to have gripped the Norman imagination; the story circulated far and wide. It was later recounted by another scribe, William of Newbridge, who recording it as fact, but who seems to have added certain embellishments. For example, he describes the land from which the children came as "St. Martin's Land" and states that its inhabitants were Christian. Other accounts state that all the inhabitants of St. Martin's Land were green in hue.

There may indeed have been feral children discovered in the forests around St. Mary's-by-the-Wolfpits in some early time, but subsequent ecclesiastical scholars have undoubtedly added their own elements to the basic tale—including the green skin coloring. It serves to demonstrate that the color green was suggestive in the Norman mind of something supernatural, unusual, or exotic, and that it was strongly connected with lush and luxuriant vegetation (such as was allegedly found in St. Martin's Land).

The idea of the color green representing the supernatural spread across Norman England with the help of the Green Children tale. Stories concerning green people (or green-clad people) were being told throughout the 12th and 13th centuries and even as late as the 14th as well. Small people, clad in green vestments, were to be seen deep in the forest glades or amongst ancient Celtic earthworks, which still littered the countryside. A fragmentary tale attributed to the conservative chronicler Richard of Devizes, a late 12th century monk at St. Swithen's house in Winchester (although perhaps not written by him at all), describes vast gatherings of green-hued people in the forest depths, where they worshipped and capered before strange gods and woodland deities. Some of these were reputedly great faces carved upon ancient stones, which imbued their followers with strange ecstasies and supernatural powers. Such goings-on, commented the chronicler, smacked of rank Witchcraft. But it was the color green that was, in his eyes, suggestive of "ancient days" and of Pagan worship; this ideal was perhaps reflected by other monks all over England. Later, the Church would lambaste such worship of "the Jack in the Green" and declare it an outright sin.

Green became the color of the fairy-kind, those who lived away from men and who were often hostile towards them, and also of the "elder races" that had dwelt in the woodlands since before the coming of "civilization." It was a color that was associated with strange magics and near-forgotten ritual. Although officially denounced by the Church, Jack in the Green (the Green Man) lingered on in the depths of men's minds and, though counted as a sin, the worship continued in secret away from the eyes of godly churchmen.

The Green Man in Christian Structures

Sin or not, this did not stop the early clerics from incorporating certain Pagan images into their holy buildings and structures. And in the medieval monasteries and parish churches, the carvings of the Green Man often acquired a special place within the building— spaces that were often allocated to special orders or functions. These included the choir and sacristy, as well as those designated for lay-men—the aisle, the transept, and the ambulatory chapels. Most of these were in the form of stone bosses, high up in the roof or decorating the apex of some high interior arch. They were also high on exterior walls, on projecting brackets, or carved on the upper areas of tombs. However, in some instances, they were also carved in wood, occasionally decorating pew ends or at the ends of misericords in the choir stalls. Of particular note were the Green Man images carved on the end of "indulgence seats" in some churches. These seats date mainly from the 14th and 15th centuries and were especially designed for aged or infirm clerics, in order to help them conduct their liturgical duties. The idea of such a Pagan image close to monks or priests performing sacred Christian ritual is especially striking.

Some of these carvings may, of course, have originated with the great families who used the churches for their acts of worship and who financially endowed the holy house in return. In the small rural medieval churches, space for the congregation was severely limited and worship was rather cramped. Many worshippers did not sit, and general seating was often restricted to a few fixed chairs for the elderly or pregnant women. The rest (similar to the monks who often remained standing through their services) were consigned to the stalls where they frequently changed position between kneeling or standing upright with heads bowed at various points in the Mass. It was not until the 15th century that a form of seating was introduced, and even then only in the shape of simple wooden benches. This, however, opened the way for more elaborate seating as the century progressed. The wealthy began to design their own elaborate seating for themselves and their families—seats with traceried backs and elaborately carved bench ends. These were then arranged to create a central aisle with the ends facing outwards so that worshippers could admire them as they passed on their way to the altar rails. The ends themselves became an expression of personal and family taste, as well as being a symbol of wealth and status. The Church tolerated such ostentatious displays as long as the individuals concerned paid well toward the upkeep of the holy house. A blind eye was sometimes turned towards carven images, which were perhaps slightly more dubious than the Church would have preferred. This included wooden heads depicting a face similar to that of the Green Man.

A number of ornamental bench ends featured what was known as the "poppy head." The name derived from the Old French *puppi* meaning a "figure head," and the carving was extremely popular in the later 14th and early to mid-15th centuries. There are more than a thousand such bench ends in the county of Somerset alone, and a number of churches in the Quantock Hills are famous for their headed pew ends, many of which included "poppy heads." Similarly, when it came to decorating the churches themselves, the financial benefactors of such an enterprise—usually the well-to-do families of the area—might also have had a personal interest in the enterprise. We have already noted how the Sinclairs conducted the interior and exterior refurbishment of Rosslyn Chapel, which lay on their estates in Scotland.

The Absence of the Green Man

Certain areas of the church, however, were exempt from such decoration and from the influence of the Green Man. The baptismal font of the medieval church, from which water was sprinkled onto the heads of infants as a token of Christ's love, had no such decoration; neither did the altar screens and pulpit. This is perhaps because they were symbolic of doctrinal and scriptural facets of the Christian religion, and their sculptures had to reflect this. Again, it may be that in these areas, the sacraments of the Church were given and these were directly connected with salvation. Quasi-Pagan effigies were, therefore, not strictly in keeping with the profound holiness of these beliefs. Thus, if there were to be decoration here, it had to be of Christ, the Apostles, or the Church fathers—symbols of propriety and sanctity.

There was also another theological debate. Some of the ornamental bosses and carvings included foliage, which surrounded the head, suggestive of spring and of vegetation. The debate raged as to whether this foliage should contain representations of fruit or flowers. This, it was argued, harked back to Pagan times when the head may well have been that of a fertility god or goddess. The inclusion of fruit or of growing things might be suggestive of the earlier

Pagan times, and was therefore to be discouraged. Therefore, in many churches and cathedrals, the Green Man is simply presented as an unadorned head. In some churches, he might be presented as a "weeper" (that is, a weeping mourner, sometimes with tears coming from his eyes) in order to get around these theological objections.

Although they were relatively popular as stone bosses and wooden bench ends, and indeed other carvings created at the whim of some beneficent family, Green Men are absent in other church mediums such as stained glass and wall paintings. Many of these were also donated to specific churches by wealthy local families of the area and all of them either carried specific Christian messages (Virgin and Child for instance) or direct depictions of scenes from the Bible (Noah's Flood, Daniel in the Lions Den, and so on). The image of the Green Man, popular though it was and symbolic of former times, had no especial religious significance within the Christian canon. But we make one exception. During the religious upheavals in England, which characterized much of the late 16th and 17th centuries, a great deal of medieval glass was destroyed and wall paintings torn down. It may be that during this period other folkloric representations of the Green Man within churches were completely removed while stone bosses and bench ends were perhaps left where they were by the Reformers. It may be too that these were actually spared because they represented a *secular* rather than a popish aspect to the church, and thus did not outrage the Reformers so much.

Protestants and the Green Man

As England formally switched from Catholicism to Protestantism during the reign of King Henry VIII (1509–1547), monasteries and other religious houses were destroyed and ransacked under the monarch's General Dissolution of the Monasteries. The King's Commissioners seized whatever they wished from the foundations— bells, chalices, relics, and anything that contained a vaguely religious image. These were often destroyed or melted down to be used elsewhere. It is possible that some of the Green Man imagery may have met this end in some parts of the country. Such iconography fared no better during the reign of Henry's feeble son Edward VI (1547–1553) when the State rigorously enforced the Anglican Church and many of the old "popish" images were destroyed.

Protestantism seems to have held a slightly ambiguous attitude toward the Green Man. On one hand, the image was one of Paganism and perhaps (in their eyes) Devil worship, while on the other hand it was not an entirely Papist symbol as, say, a representation of the Virgin might be. Protestantism (and by association the Puritanism that arose in England during the 17th century) may not have identified the figure as a specific religious threat and may have been prepared to tolerate it. Indeed, William Anderson, in his book *The Green Man* (1990) identifies an example of the image being used as a printer's mark on certain Protestant texts in Europe. The works in question included Bibles and theological treatises, and the figure appeared in border design, on the colophons of chapters, and one actually appears on a printed title page of Luther's *Appalatio ad Concillion* (*Appeal to the Council*) dated from 1530. This important Protestant work is illustrated with a foliate head with vegetation issuing from its nostrils that blossoms into greenery and flowers. To the left of this head stands the figure of an admonishing preacher with a finger raised, and to the right a woman reading a book, which may be a religious treatise or the Bible.

Man in the Oak

It would appear therefore that, despite the stereotypical notions some historians, Protestants, similar to their Catholic counterparts, used the iconography of the Green Man within their own religious framework, at least in some European circles.

This is not to say, however, that all aspects of the Green Man were readily accepted by the Protestant administrations. During the Interregnum in England in the mid-17th century (the period of the English Commonwealth 1649–59) the rural celebrations, which heralded the beginning of spring, together with all other traditional festivals, were forbidden. Successive Puritan-led parliaments viewed such gatherings with a deep distrust, which may have been actually more from a political standpoint than a religious one. Nevertheless, there was a generally held religious perception amongst the Puritans that the populace should be concentrating on their Bibles and on the worship of God instead of dancing in rituals or celebrating some ancient and traditional festival. The Puritans, of course, had their own reasons for their antagonism towards the Green Man—or "the Man in the Oak"—because King Charles I had been found hiding in an oak tree to escape capture in 1647 as the English Civil War drew to a close. The connection between the monarch in the tree and the King of the Wood may not have been lost upon the Puritan people. The Nominated Assembly of Saints, or Barebones Parliament of 1653 (which took its title from the splendidly named preacher Praise God Barebones), which paved the way for the English Protectorate and the rise of Oliver Cromwell, passed a number of enactments preventing traditional rural gatherings such as Maypole Dancing or Jack in the Green on pain of imprisonment or even death for the participants. Local ministers, appointed by an office of the Parliament, often acted as informers in an effort to suppress such revels. But despite these strict edicts and possibly in spite of informers, many of these festivals connected to the Green Man continued in remote rural areas. Many were conducted in secret, adding to the air of mystery that already surrounded this iconic figure.

We must be careful, however, not to assume that England was a country of rustic peasantry who unquestioningly (if secretly) accepted old and traditional ways, dancing around Maypoles and holding festivals in their rural seclusion. Indeed, there were those in rural areas who openly dismissed such perceptions as "false superstitions."

In the late 16th century, the Kentish squire, Reginald Scot, in his book *The Discoverie of Witchcraft* (published in 1584), listed and summarily dismissed a range of figures about which he had heard in his boyhood. Scot's purpose in writing the book was to hopefully bring to an end the Witch persecutions that had sprung up following the religious fluctuations between Catholicism (in the reign of Mary I) and Protestantism (in the reign of Elizabeth I) by disproving the existence of Witchcraft both as an individual supernatural act and as an organized secretive and subversive "religion" based in early folk practices. Amongst some of the figures he lists (and often pokes fun at) are Robin Goodfellow, the wodewose, and the Man in the Oak—all aspects of the Green Man (although it is notable that in the late 16th century they were seen as three distinct figures). Scot heaps scorn on all three, utterly dismissing them as "rank superstition," and stating that they were only the beliefs of the "credulous and the gullible."

Although writing in the 16th century, the squire was perhaps the forerunner of a new style of thinking. It was a type of thinking that moved away from the folkloric elements of society and towards a more scientifically based perspective. It was the style of thinking that would characterize what came to be known as the Enlightenment. Such thinking consigned that which could not be scientifically proven to the realms of credulity and foolishness. This included reliance on old gods and old ways, amongst them the Green Man.

Once again, we must be careful here because it would be inaccurate to say that belief in the old ways and old images died out completely. Although the period of the Puritan Parliament and the new scientifically orientated thinking may have changed some rural perspectives, it is safe to assume that at least some of the old traditions and festivals continued in certain areas. However, it is probably also safe to assume that ancient beliefs were probably not carried out with the same enthusiasm. The era of the Green Man, preeminent in medieval times, was passing. The times were changing and so were beliefs.

Resurrection of the Green Man

It was arguably the 19th and early 20th centuries that brought the image back to prominence again; here the notion of the Green Man began to subtly change. Previously, it had been viewed as a Pagan symbol, connected to a superstitious and rather wild past—it was a symbol of fertility and earthiness. The Victorians, however, with a slight sense of romance, changed all that. The 1800s were characterized by an interest in and a nostalgia for the simplicity of previous eras. These were sometimes viewed in a highly romantic light—perhaps as a reaction to the intense scientific preoccupations of former years. The latter half of the 19th century saw a growing interest in "ancient mysteries," in vanished races and civilizations, and in ancient monoliths and structures, which were still to be found in various parts of the world.

Attention was now turned to accounts of ancient festivals, some of which were believed to have an occult significance. Indeed, an interest in the occult and the supernatural appeared to be growing once more in the Victorian mind. This interest would continue well into the early 20th century. There was, for example, a growing interest in the Far East—particularly in the remote kingdoms of the Himalayas, such as Tibet, which were believed to hold secrets that had been lost to modern science. Egypt was said to hold a number of secrets, which had been long forgotten by the Western world. This led to much excavation around the Valley of Kings there in the early 20th century. The fascination with former worlds now seemed endless. And for many English, there were also interests closer to home.

Forgotten Secrets

Across the country during the latter years of the 19th century, there was great interest in stone circles and standing stones, many dating from prehistoric times, that hinted at the secrets and mysteries of long-vanished races. The rising interest in the occult and Spiritualism quickly tapped into this idea. Such places were the center of ancient forces, which had existed since the very dawn of time. The medieval world had known the truth of such things, but the modern world had either forgotten or, for its own reasons, proscribed such knowledge. We have already noted how certain churches—such as Rosslyn Chapel in Scotland—were reputedly built at the junctures of certain lines of ancient force, known as ley lines.

These forces were natural and belonged to an earlier era when ancient gods supposedly ruled the world. Implicit in this was the desire, even in the staid Victorian mind, to be reunited with the energies of Nature and with the Natural world.

Certain special and secretive societies were formed, many with the purpose of exploring the ancient natural and mystical forces of the countryside. More importantly, many ancient festivals that had lain dormant in men's memories since the 17th century now were revived, especially in rural villages and towns. Once again, an interest was shown in Morris men dancing and the figure of the Green Man or Jack in the Green. Figures clothed in leaves and vegetation began to reappear at gatherings, which were held all over England, as the Victorians seemed to rediscover their mythic roots and Maypole dancing became a feature of many village festivals. In places such as the Peak District, ceremonies were held for the Garland King and Queen, surely an echo of some former time, while in the North of England, Jack in the Wad (perhaps Jack in the Wood—a variation of Jack in the Green) also made an appearance in several locations. All of these figures were accompanied by Morris dancers and a retinue of lesser characters—perhaps representing lesser nature deities and spirits.

Some of these festivals claimed origins from the Restoration of the King, Charles II, in 1660—presumably to give them some form of legitimacy—and were described as "Oak Tree Festivals" after the king's father who had been found hiding in an oak tree. However, their significance may well have been far older. Indeed, in the late 1700s and into the early 1800s, such festivals were appearing all over the English countryside and Scotland as well. For example, in

South Queensferry on the Firth of Forth, roughly 10 miles from Edinburgh, a figure known as the Burry Man—a creature swathed in vegetation and wearing a skirt of leaves, made an appearance. This fantastic creature may have originally been connected with vegetation, but also with plentiful supplies of fish, because similar figures are also found with some local characteristics in other Scottish coastal fishing villages such as Fraserborough. On the Island of Arran too, fantastic figures used to appear at certain times of the year representing the Celtic sea god Shony, and at these times a cask of beer was often thrown into the ocean as an offering, or a bottle of whiskey poured on the waves. Some folklorists have argued that beings akin to the Burry Man, in both England and Scotland, served as some sort of scapegoats who were supposedly ceremonially sacrificed and took away the evils of the community, thus ensuring good harvests, or in the case of a coastal community, excellent catches. An entire day of festivities was centered on such figures, lasting from sunrise to sunset; if this were not observed then the community would not prosper for at least a year afterward.

May Day

An important time for these gatherings was May Day (May 1). This, of course, gives a clue as to the antiquity of such beliefs because the first day of May was also the ancient Celtic feast of Beltane (or Beltaine), the start of the summer. This was also the time, in folkloric circles, of the "greenwood marriage"—when young men and women took partners in open-air pairings, in the style of the old Celtic handfast weddings. It was a time of union and procreation, and fit in well with many of the ideas of the Green Man. In some of these ceremonies, during the 19th and early 20th centuries,

A Greenwood Marriage

it was common for some of the participants to wear leaf-green masks in honor of the "woodland deities" or "good folk" (fairies). Once again, this provided a tangible link with Nature, if only for a day.

The central figure of these May Day festivals was the King (or latterly Queen) of the May. It may be that the beginning of summer was the time when the ancient King of the Wood was ritually sacrificed to ensure a good harvest at summer's end, and the idea of the King of the May was some sort of folkloric memory of that. It may also be that the May King was also another name for Jack in the Green or the Green Man, as he was feted and venerated in almost regal style for the entire day. Other names for the May King were the Garland Man, Mad Jack, John Barleycorn (a corn deity), or John of the Wold.

Historical Figures

Historical figures also appeared in many communities. Reference has already been made to the Restoration of King Charles II—the symbolic restoration of the monarchy after the Cromwellian period—who appeared in some rural gatherings as the "Oak King," but there were others as well. For instance, in parts of County Tipperary in Ireland, the figure of Gerald Fitzgerald, 13th Earl of Desmond is central to certain celebrations. Earl Gerald is generally known in Irish folklore as "the Wizard Earl," and was said to have lived in an enchanted castle beneath the waters of Lough Gur in County Limerick. The actual historical figure of the earl is something of an enigma and is probably associated with early Irish alchemy. Earl Gerald, who lived in the 16th century, was probably something of a scientist or a chemist, activities that were often considered as Witchcraft in these early modern times. During his investigations, he was supposed to have discovered the Emerald Tablet which, if ground down and consumed in a glass of wine, would enable the drinker to live forever. Each year, according to legend, he is supposed to ride out from his underwater castle and carry off the prettiest girl, the strongest man, or the most intelligent scholar to live with him under Lough Gur. At other times, he simply appears and tries to inveigle away people from the countryside to his deep abode—and there are many tales of those who have encountered him. Over the years, he also became a kind of Nature spirit, and this may explain his association with the communal festivals in such places as Tipperary. His appearance at various festivals was also supposed to bring good luck for the coming year.

In some areas, the historical figures of Wat Tyler and Jack Straw were also featured, although this aspect seems to have died out rather quickly. Both Tyler and Straw were leaders of the English Peasant's Revolt of 1381 during the reign of King Richard II, and were believed to have an affinity with the agricultural laborers and therefore, by association, with Nature. Through the years, both of them may well have become folk heroes, margining into the mythology of a number of rural communities—whether they were directly connected to them or not—and thus became central to local festivals.

The Green Man in Present Day

From Victorian times onward, large numbers of ancient festivals were revived, some to generate a sense of community spirit and some, latterly, to bring in tourism and boost the economy of relatively deprived areas. Even as late as the 1970s, community festivals were still emerging based around folklore themes and with the Green

Man—or some similar figure—at their center. Customs that had sometimes lain dormant for years now began to reemerge once more as part of the celebrations. For example, the Milkmaids' Garlands—wreaths of flowers and other greenery given to milkmaids on May 1—were very common in Essex during the early 19th century. In return, the prettiest milkmaids had to dance a small jig for their customers. The custom was revived around the 1960s but this time, the Garland was made from pewter and was presented by the King or Queen of the May (or some other such figure—for example Jack in the Green) to the prettiest girl who worked in the dairy industry. Similarly, in places such as the village of Abbotsbury, in Dorset, a number of Shepherds' Garlands were presented each year on the May 13, at a local gathering. Garlands also played a large part in communal life there. The folklorist and Edwardian Member of Parliament, Sir Benjamin Stone, photographed the celebrations and recorded the following:

> On the 13th of May, usually known as "Garland Day," the children go around the village with large garlands, soliciting gifts of money from householders. After they have called on all the inhabitants, they proceed to the beach. Then the garlands are placed in boats and, instead of being committed to the waves, as they used to be, and as such tributes still are in several of the Greek islands, brought back again. This is a recent innovation. So also is the ecclesiastical character now given to the festival—the children taking the garlands to church, where a special service is held—before they are carried out to sea in the boats.

It is, indeed, dying out. Of old a dozen or more boats, each with a garland, put off from the shore at Abbotsbury, as against one from Swyre and another from Puncknowle [both of these are nearby local villages near the Chesil] and every floral offering was placed on the waves in the firm belief that it would bring back the mackerel fishing. But latterly only two or three boats have gone to sea.

Days similar to the Garland Day which Stone refers were generally treated as a general holiday by the entire community—just as they had been treated as a communal festival by previous generations. However, certain things had changed. With these various revivals, a certain religious element had now crept in. The festivals were now, in the main, no longer simply seen as continuations of the Pagan ceremonies of antiquity but rather, perhaps, as an extension of Christian worship. After all, God was the originator of fertility and fruitfulness, so why should He not be worshipped through old customs? As Stone notes, the garlands that had originally been sacrificed on the tides were now taken into the church for a service of Christian blessing before being consigned to the deep. This new style of thinking and perception would give the Green Man a slightly different angle. Rather than being a dark and Pagan character—a reminder of ancient human sacrifice—he became rather more acceptable, a symbol of communal and religious unity. The head of the Green Man was now a reminder of a much more innocent and cohesive time when societies had worked together both for the good of themselves and for the good of Nature. All the former anxieties concerning the image seem to have been glossed over.

This new ethos allowed the Green Man once again to appear in church decoration. He was now the symbol of the harvest, of fruitfulness, of God's bounty. With the new interest in Gothic architecture and the rather bizarre and arcane, the idea of the foliate head, concealed in nooks and crannies, fit in well. In a number of new and refurbished churches and cathedrals dating from the 1800s, the Green Man once more makes an appearance. However, he was probably not regarded as the King of the Wood, the monarch who ritually laid down his life, but as the Lord of Harvest, through whom God bestowed His graciousness on His followers. He now became a symbol of goodness and wholesomeness.

And yet it would be wrong to assume that the Green Man had changed completely overnight, for there were probably still suspicions and doubts regarding the figure and its inclusion in church architecture in many Christian minds. At least some memories of the Green Man's Pagan past still lingered in the back of godly minds and created uncertainty and distrust. Nevertheless, the Green Man appeared as ornamentation once again in many Victorian places of worship. They became part of wall-brackets and on the outer walls as decorative waterspouts to accompany gargoyles that were already there. These uses were considered to be much more functional and acceptable and could not claim to be "centering" ancient Pagan powers within church precincts.

The changed, "more acceptable" perception of the Green Man gradually spread out into the wider community. No more was Jack in the Green seen as a sinister relic of the Pagan times, but rather as a community figure around which churches and town and village councils could base fetes and community parties. He became more akin to the Santa Claus figure (who ironically had probably also started out as a figure of wildness and veneration in pre-Christian times). Furthermore, his association with Nature and the Natural world gave him an air of wholesomeness and concern for the overall planet.

Politics and the Green Man

It is not a coincidence therefore, that the political movement that concerned itself with Natural conservation and the protection of Natural resources chose the color green as its emblem. The Green Movement (and latterly its formally political expression—the Green Party) is well-known in many Western countries in relation to lobbying on conservation and preservation issues. "Green politics" has now become an accepted term in the European political landscape, with many politicians anxious to show their "green credentials." In America too, there is a green movement but during the presidency of George W. Bush this has, perhaps, not been as effective as it might have been due to Washington's deliberate blocking of certain issues in order to sustain corporate financial gain. However, with issues such as global warming gradually creeping up the political agenda, "green politics" is more and more coming to the fore. Today, green has become the color of concern, of social conscience, and perhaps "trendiness."

Health and the Green Man

The Jolly Green Giant

In one instance, the Green Man became a symbol of health and natural goodness by taking on another persona. He became the Jolly Green Giant, an advertising icon used by the Green Giant

Food Company, based in Sueur, Minnesota. The Green Giant was originally used in 1928 to sell a range of vegetable products (primarily peas) by pointing out that they were completely natural and wholesome. To do this he was portrayed as a green-skinned titan, dressed in skins, with a foliate crown and boots made from leaves. By using such an image, the Green Giant (already a successful vegetable product company) emphasised the freshness and goodness of its products. The campaign was a roaring success and soon the company was able to open canning plants in Cokato, Montgomery, and Winstead Minnesota.

The voice of the Green Giant, who later appeared in radio and television advertisements, was former jazz singer Len Dresslar, who died on October 16, 2005. Dresslar was something of a giant himself, standing well over 6 feet tall, and was able to actually portray the giant with his deep "ho-ho-hoing" laugh during television campaigns. Sometimes, he was accompanied by a human-sized companion called Sprout, again emphasising growing and Natural things. Both radio and television campaigns were particularly successful and the Jolly Green Giant soon became accepted as part of American culture. Today, the Jolly Green Giant is a universally accepted symbol of natural goodness and of healthy wholesomeness. In fact, he has become part of the American psyche.

Johnny Appleseed

It has been argued that the advertisers based the Giant on an old American legend—that of the giant Johnny Appleseed. In a sense, Johnny Appleseed was the closest America to having its old "wild man of the forests," and though folklore has often portrayed him as a giant, he was in fact based on a real human being.

John Chapman was born in Massachusetts on September 26, 1774 into a Revolutionary family. His father, Nathaniel Chapman, fought with the Minutemen at Concord in 1775. It is possible that when Johnny was born, he suffered from a condition known today as Marfan syndrome, a genetic disorder in which a sufferer could have abnormally long limbs. Although there is little information about his life, it is known that John Chapman was deeply religious and that he became a missionary in the Church of New Jerusalem, a Christian sect who followed the Biblical interpretations of Emmanuel Swedenborg, a Swedish theologian.

As a farmer, John Chapman was interested in fruit, particularly apples. Apples formed a central part of the New England diet. For example, they could be used to make hard cider and applejack, which were the preferred drinks of some of the early colonists. Dried apple segments known as snitz could also be used for flavoring stews and soups in colonial cooking, and also formed the basis of snitz and knep—a pork/smoked bacon and apple dish much beloved of German immigrants.

In 1797, John Chapman struck westward, following the line of the pioneer trails, and it is here that fact merges into folklore. It is said that he went into the uncharted territories, planting apple trees from seed as he went. This gave him his famous nickname of Appleseed. It is also said that he lived in the wild, amongst the Indians. It is quite possible that, given his pacifist religious views, he acted as an intermediary between settlers and Indians concerning land deals. As time went on and folklore concerning him developed, he became the archetypical wild man, living in the forests, planting trees, and conversing with Nature. John Chapman died on March 18, 1854 in Fort Wayne, Indiana, leaving behind a wealth of folklore. Tales would transform him into a wild but ultimately friendly giant (he was probably quite tall in any case, given his physical condition) who was more an embodiment of the forests through which he moved. A symbol of kindliness and natural goodness, it is quite possible that the folkloric connection aided the promotion of the Jolly Green Giant in the American mind and consequently made the advertising campaign all the more successful.

Literature and the Green Man

Literature too has taken the Green Man to its heart and given the image a more respectable gloss. Books and poetry explored the tensions between religion and Paganism through the medium of the image, and developed themes that had been raised in earlier writings. For instance, *The Green Helmet*, written by the celebrated Irish poet W.B. Yeats seems to have, in part, been based upon the Irish Celtic legend of Bricrui's Feast, which, in turn, contained some of the themes found in *Sir Gawain and the Green Knight*. A later novel by a renowned author—Irish Murdoch's *The Green Knight*—is also loosely based on the same medieval work. One of the central characters, for example, carries a green umbrella and is linked to the knight of the earlier story by several other characters in the book. Famous anthropological works, such as the already-mentioned Sir James Frazer's *The Golden Bough* also dealt directly with the idea of the Green Man, while it may have influenced poetry such as T.S. Eliot's *The Waste Land,* which holds some of the themes regarding the tension between humans and Nature.

The notion of such reputable writers writing directly about or being influenced by the image, leant a certain amount of credibility and respectability to the Green Man. This list of famous authors also included English writer Sir Kingsley Amis in his supernatural horror novel directly entitled *The Green Man.* The novel was later turned into a highly successful English television drama and has provided the basis for a number of stage-plays as well, firmly establishing the Green Man in a cultural context. The image has appeared in numerous other works of fiction either as a main protagonist or as a subplot.

Comic Books

It was a relatively small step from the written word in text form to a comic book format. Arguably, one of the earliest incarnations of the Green Man—the wild and unbiddible force of Nature—was *The Incredible Hulk,* created by Marvel Comics in the early 1960s. Here, an intelligent and sophisticated scientist, Bruce Banner, was accidentally transformed by an exploding gamma-ray bomb into a marauding green titan known as the Hulk. The idea was far from the friendly, wholesome concept of the Jolly Green Giant. Although the strip's creator, Stan Lee, has argued that the concept owes perhaps more to Robert Louis Stevenson's classic novel *Dr. Jeckyll and Mr. Hyde,* there are still some elements of the Green Man scattered about. First, the Hulk is an ambiguous being containing two distinct elements within him. For part of the time, he was the distinguished, intellectual scientist, Bruce Banner, and at other times, he was the raw, brutal, rampaging Hulk. The Hulk was also green in color and, in this respect, represented an uncontrolled nature. Banner spent his time trying to reunite the twin aspects of the character.

The *Incredible Hulk* rapidly became on of Marvel's top-selling titles and is still one of the company's flagship characters. So successful did it become that between the years 1977 and 1982, it ran as a popular television series, starring veteran actor Bill Bixby as Dr. Bruce Banner and body-builder Lou Ferrigno as his brutal and rampaging counterpart. Although the series finished in 1982, it was re-screened in the form of repeats all over America and in other countries besides, thus ensuring that its popularity didn't die out. Later, in 2003, celebrated film director Ang Lee (director of *Crouching Tiger, Hidden Dragon* and later *Brokeback Mountain)* directed a Hulk film, starring Eric Bana and Jennifer Connolly, and using state-of-the-art computer graphics, which was moderately successful but somewhat failed to capture the excitement of the original comic strip.

The Hulk was not Marvel's only creation in the field. As a response to the success of *Swamp Thing*, the creation of rival DC Comics, Lee, together with writers Roy Thomas and Gerry Conway brought Man-Thing into being. With artist Gray Morrow, the character appeared in Marvel's *Savage Tales #1* as a kind of science fiction entity. Dr. Ted Sallis, a bioengineer, had discovered a new formula for creating a chemically based life form. Unfortunately, a super-criminal organization—Advanced Idea Mechanics (A.I.M), an organization that had appeared in several other Marvel titles— also wished to acquire the basic formula that Sallis kept in a container. While fleeing A.I.M., Sallis drove into the Florida swamplands where he was drowned in a swamp, taking the formula with him. This kept him alive by turning him into the Man-Thing, a massive muck-monster that roamed through the Everglades on a quest to regain its lost humanity. Similar to the Hulk, the Man-Thing only seemed to have a limited intelligence, but was treated as a god by members of a nearby Seminole Reservation. It was the archetypical "creature from the swamp."

Sales of the Man-Thing as a title were reasonable-to-low and so a new writer, Steve Gerber, was brought in from *Savage Tales #14* to give the character a shot in the arm. Initially, the Man-Thing had been a science fiction character, something similar to a mucky Frankenstein, but Gerber introduced a raft of new ideas, including demons, supernatural warriors, and time-traveling adventurers. This type of plot was developed by a number of subsequent writers and an artist named Chris Claremont, who began to cross over the Man-Thing with another Marvel title—*Dr. Strange*. Claremont also introduced an H.P. Lovecraft-type theme, which was moderately successful but didn't really lift sales as Marvel had hoped.

With so many writers and so many plot lines, the Man-Thing's basic character had also slightly changed. His intelligence began to fluctuate between extremely limited and highly intellectual. From time to time, the creature assumed supernatural powers. Many fans began to find Clairmont's plot lines rather ludicrous, sales dipped, and the magazine was discontinued, with the Man-Thing finishing his adventures in *Doctor Strange #2*. However, the character didn't die, but kept reappearing in a number of other Marvel titles.

For instance, Man-Thing appeared fighting the Hulk and again in *Spider-Man* and *Daredevil* as well as *Dr. Strange* and the flagship *X-Men*.

Similar to the Hulk before it, the Man-Thing was also made into a film in 2005, directed by Brett Leonard and starring Matthew le Nevez and Rachael Taylor. Both the characters and plot were somewhat changed to fit into a more modern idiom, and bore little resemblance to the original strip. It was something of a disappointment at the box office and passed most of the filmgoing public by.

By far the most successful of all the muck/swamp monsters, however, was the *Swamp Thing* (on which Marvel's Man-Thing had been based) created for Marvel's rival, DC Comic, by Len Wein and Bernie Wrightson. This creature had started out as a one-off story in the company's popular title *House of Secrets*. In the original story, published in June–July 1971, the protagonist was Dr. Alex Olsen, a chemical researcher, killed in an explosion organized by his assistant Damian Ridge, so that Ridge could attempt to gain the hand of Olsen's wife Linda. However, the will to live, combined with the chemicals his body had absorbed as a result of the explosion, turned him into a shambling muck-monster with incredible strength. Linda had resisted Ridge's overtures, and so the murderous assistant planned to do away with her as well. However, recognizing what Ridge was up to, Olsen as the muck-monster killed him. Unable to make Linda realize who he was, the muck-man shambled away into the swamps, never to be seen again—or so the writers and publishers thought.

The story, however, proved a hit with readers who wanted to see more, and so Wein and Wrightson were brought in to design a new title for DC The title they created was *Swamp Thing*, launched in October–November 1972. In this, Dr. Alex Olsen changed his name to Dr. Alec Holland but was still metamorphosised into a muck-creature as the result of a chemical explosion, although this time the conflagration was created by an "enemy agent" known as Mr. E. The formula, which he absorbed, was a kind of vegetation-based chemical, designed to restore growth to barren areas of the world. His determination to live, combined with the properties of the chemicals, served to create the Swamp Thing, which shambled off into the swamplands of Louisiana. There were differences, however, between the two incarnations of the Swamp Thing—the major one being that the later had a limited mode of speech (lack of speech had been the primary reason why Dr. Alex Olsen had been unable to communicate who he was to his wife). The entity was also far more muscular than its *House of Secrets* counterpart.

At the outset, the title proved incredibly popular and ran, in its first series, from 1972 until 1976, with Bernie Wrightson as artist and Len Wein controlling writing and the plotline. The story followed the usual DC format, pitting the Swamp Thing against a string of fairly standard supervillains, the most interesting being Dr. Anton Arcane, who made several appearances. Sales of the title began to plummet towards the end of the first series, and DC made a change of both writer and artist.

The new team, David Michelinie and Gerry Conway, tried a number of approaches to revive the flagging series, including introducing space aliens and sorcerers, together with the introduction of Holland's brother, but nothing could reverse the title's decline. In the end, they allowed Alec Holland to regain his human form and the series closed early in 1977.

In 1982, interest in the Swamp Thing was rekindled by a film directed by legendary Hollywood figure Wes Craven. Although the film was not a huge success and is now largely forgotten, it did inspire DC to relaunch the title. A new series was commissioned under the title *Saga of the Swamp Thing,* with Martin Pasko as its writer. Initial reader reaction was very favorable but soon began to fall off again. In this series, the effects of Holland's "humanization" were discovered to be only a temporary state, and very soon he reverted to being the muck-monster Swamp Thing once more. Although several new villains were brought in, Swamp Thing went once more into what seemed to be terminal decline.

With the series scheduled for closure again, DC brought in an English writer, the then largely unknown Alan Moore. It was Moore who gave the Swamp Thing a more mystical but intensely darker character, which found favor with many of the readership. Although essentially human, the Swamp Thing would from time to time slip into a dimension known as "The Green," which connected all the vegetable world. As well as this idea, Moore introduced a villain who had roughly the same properties as the Swamp Thing itself—Floronic Man—who held a grudge against the human world. Moore redefined the Swamp Thing not as a kind of superhero, but as a mystical, supernatural creature, turning the title into a horror comic—one of the first since the DC titles of the 1950s.

Swamp Thing established his name in the field of comics and also changed the way in which comics were perceived—no longer as entertainment fodder but rather as valid literature. The series laid the basis for DC's Vertigo imprint, which often featured darker themes than were to be found in mainstream comics. Moore also began to introduce a "mythos"-type approach to comic-book writing, founding DC's supernatural universe, which was developed later by such writer/artists as Neil Gaiman. In a sense, the Alan Moore period was one of the series' highpoints and showed the Swamp Thing as a continuation of folkloric themes and storytelling tradition.

Alan Moore stopped working on the Swamp Thing in 1987 and was succeeded by a number of writers and artists, none of whom really achieved the success of the title in the early 1980s. These included Nancy Collins, Mark Millar, Rick Veitch, and Doug Wheeler. Veitch, who was Moore's successor on the series, maintained many of the themes that Moore had started and also increasingly introduced crossover plots into other DC titles. This series would run until the last week of 1999 when, with Millar as its writer, Swamp Thing was again discontinued as an independent title by DC The creature would continue to occasionally make an appearance in some of the company's other titles but no new series was planned.

A third series, however, did appear due to public pressure, penned by Brian K. Vaughan between 2000 and 2001. This actually featured the daughter of the Swamp Thing and was not all that successful. Again the series was discontinued and the Swamp Thing was put into abeyance once more, making the odd guest appearance in a number of DC titles including *Superman*.

A fourth (and current) series was commissioned in 2004. The writer is now Joshua Dysart, who has returned the Swamp Thing to its original muck-monster status with much of Alec Holland's humanity lost. The series will likely not continue beyond the end of 2006/beginning of 2007, due to relatively low sales and the appeals of die-hard fans. From time to time, however, popular interest in the character revives, so there may well be a fifth series scheduled for some future date.

Although Man-Thing and Swamp Thing were the best-known muck-creatures, due to marketing by their respective comic companies, they were not the only ones. As early as 1942, such beings were making an appearance. In that year Airboy Comics released the *Heap* title, in which a German World War I pilot crashed into a bog and through his sheer will to live, became one with the surrounding morass that seemed to be possessed of a mystical force. Image Comics briefly revived the character in the mid-1990s. Other mud-monsters included Berni Wrightson's aptly named Muck Monster that made a single appearance in *Eerie 68* (September 1975); a slime character which rose out of a bog in DC's *Phantom Stranger* during the mid-1970s; *Sludge* from Malibu Comics in 1993, which featured a policeman accidentally turned into a hideous mud-creature while fleeing from the Mafia through a swamp; Eclipse's 1987 series *Elf-Thing,* which was simply a take-off of all other such monsters, including Swamp Thing and which featured a killer elf; right through to the Atlas Comic's *Bog Beast* (Atlas Comics 1974); and Scott Shaw's early 1970s muck-monster parody *Turd.*

Even some British weekly comics got in on the act when IPC released *The Blob* in the late 1960s, although this was more of a cautionary tale about the perceived evils of nuclear energy and toxic nuclear waste than anything else. The Blob here was little more than a menacing and unintelligent shape drifting in from the ocean, and the strip was a straightforward action story.

Both the Swamp Thing and Man-Thing, as well as some of the other such comic-strip creatures reveal, in the context of popular, modern culture, the deep and subconscious yearnings that have underpinned the myth of the Green Man across the centuries. The fusion of swamp (Nature) and Man into a single entity clearly symbolizes the union of Mankind with the surrounding world. The fury of the Hulk and the almost supernatural strength of other such characters emphasises the wildness that Mankind has supposedly left behind but which still exists, deep down, in all of us. His unreasoning rage against the mechanized, modern world perhaps symbolises the same alienation we sometimes feel towards a bland and often unfeeling society. But perhaps it was the Alan Moore period of the Swamp Thing title that most clearly underscored this with its emphasis on the supernatural and on ancient mysteries—the basis of the belief in Jack in the Green or the Green Man. There is still a notion, locked away in some almost forgotten part of our mind that old and powerful forces might still exist and that they can be experienced through the often-overwhelming power of raw Nature. Despite our seeming intelligence and sophistication, there is still an element of the primitive in us all, and it is this that sometimes emerges through our culture. It is this too that may explain our interest in and fascination with the Green Man in whatever form the image takes, whether it be a medieval stone boss in a rural church, or a comic book on the newsstand on the side of the busy street. In many incarnations, it is one of our most enduring images and one that touches us all at the deepest level.

Conclusion

The image of the Green Man has had a long, tortuous, and complicated journey through the centuries—from early perceptions of forest, corn, and vegetation gods, through medieval stone carvings in churches and other sites, to modern day comic books and films. And although it is primarily associated with early Celtic civilizations (especially that of England), there are varying echoes of a similar image and perception in other cultures. Indeed, it is quite possible that no other icon has survived for so long in the human consciousness, or has taken on so many incarnations.

This resilience across the ages only serves to demonstrate the importance of the foliate head as one of our deepest psychological images. As we have seen, it denotes a yearning that lies at the very core of our collective being—a yearning to be reunited with and to be seen as a part of Nature. This yearning, of course, as we have noted, has manifested itself in other folkloric ways—in tales of a lost, innocent world; in descriptions of some vague Otherworld or lost paradise, such as the Garden of Eden or the Land of

Eternal Youth; in ideas of marvelous but now vanished civilizations. But the foliate head has always been a tangible and *physical* representation of such a longing.

We have also seen that the Green Man may have, in some of its earliest incarnations, been exclusively male. In fact, the foliate male head may well have been an interpretation of the Great Mother from whose womb everything in the world was deemed to have sprung and who was sometimes characterized by images such as the Irish Sheela-na-gig. And in some of the festivals celebrating spring or the beginning of summer, female entities sometimes make an appearance—such as the May Queen on May Day. In fact, it is quite possible that the head wreathed by foliage replaced the vagina of the early images of prehistoric female goddesses who represented fertility. Such a representation may well have been more acceptable to the Christian clerics who were to come later.

The connections that formed around the Green Man icon were, in a sense, similar to those associated with Christianity. The head of the Green Man represented sacrifice for the common good and well-being; there were ideas too of resurrection and rebirth, the return of the crops, and the coming once again of springtime and harvest each year. Christianity, in common with many of the other Middle Eastern cults, held such ideas as a central belief. Christ, similar to the King of the Wood who was sacrificed so that the crops would grow every year, had also died to cleanse the world of evil and imperfection, and to ensure salvation for His followers. This similarity meant that some elements of the Green Man belief might be assimilated into the Christian message and into Christian imagery.

From roughly the 12th century onwards, foliate heads appeared in the decoration of Christian churches. If there were any used before that, there is no evidence of them. However, between the 1300s and the mid-1500s, images of the Green Man seem to appear in church decoration—both in stone bosses and in wooden bench-ends—with remarkable frequency, particularly in England. It was the General Dissolution of the Monasteries under the English king Henry VIII, coupled with the English Civil War and the rise of the Commonwealth, which seems to have put an end to such decorative images in the country; it would lie dormant until the later Victorian era when it would emerge once more.

On the Continent, however, the idea of the Green Man seemed to continue. The fact that it had been tenuously linked with Pagan ritual or with certain heretical orders, such as the Templars, hardly seemed to matter. The emergent Continental Protestantism saw it as little threat, and while it no longer graced either the interior or exterior of churches, it did appear on certain Protestant religious pamphlets and publications as an imprint. Throughout the centuries, the religious attitude toward the image always seems to have appeared to be somewhat ambivalent.

During the Victorian age in England, the idea of the Green Man enjoyed something of a renaissance; there were probably three interconnected reasons for this. First, a notion of rural romance, which manifested itself in the works of poets such as John Keats, or in the paintings of John Constable, pervaded the time. This was complemented by the music of such English composers as Vaughan Williams, and the art of Sir Edward Elgar, who painted atmospheric and leisurely melodic pictures suggestive of a pleasant country life. This created a kind of English rural idyll in the Victorian mind, suggestive of woodlands, growth, harvest, and so on—things that might well be associated with folklore and the Green Man. With

Summer Queen

increasing industrialization and urbanization, such a perception may well have seemed ever more appealing to the English Victorian mind. And although much of this seems to have occurred in England (possibly because of the emphasis on English art), it was matched elsewhere in Europe.

As cities such as Paris continued to grow and expand, its inhabitants often looked more towards the French countryside in both art and literature. Such thinking and perception was fertile ground for an interest in traditions such as the Green Man. Second, it was a part of the general mood of enquiry of the time. Throughout the 18th and early 19th centuries, there had been significant steps forward in a number of scientific and industrial fields. Having partially explored the world around them, some Victorians now turned their attention towards the past. This was still an age of enquiry, exploration, and adventure, and while some could go off to open up foreign lands, others stayed at home and explored the traditions and myths of the landscape around them. Thirdly, the foliate head represented a tangible appeal to the past. Already some Victorian explorers were finding other societies deep in the jungles of Africa and South America who were apparently untouched by "civilization." There were also Indians living on the plains of America whose culture was also being uncovered. Although regarded as primitives by Victorian culture, there was something virginal and unspoiled— and intensely more honest—about these cultures. These were the true, innocent children of Nature who lived in harmony with their world, the way that all men had in eons long past. In some respects they were the counterbalance to the cynicism, commercialism, greed, and outright corruption that sometimes characterized the industrialized world. The myth of the "Noble Savage"—unsullied and uncorrupted by the concerns of "civilization"—was already forming in the Victorian perception. The way in which many of these "primitive" peoples integrated with their surroundings reignited the yearning deep within the industrialized, urbanized, and mechanized individuals.

The foliate head, with its long history and knowing look, often provided a focus for all of these elements. Thus it began to reemerge in the Victorian world and new sculpture and decoration took notice of it once more. It became the center of an exploration into the traditions and myths of the past. This "renaissance" not only took the form of stylized decorations, but also of many fairs and festivals, many of which had not been in evidence since the time of the English Commonwealth or the dawn of the Enlightenment. And at their center was Jack in the Green, the Green Man, or some similar figure who presided over the festival and bestowed good fortune and well-being on all the participants.

A number of these festivals have survived down to the present day, although now they are regarded more as community gatherings than congregations of dark and Pagan worshippers. In fact, many have become tourist and communal attractions designed to bring in tourists and enhancing the local economies of their respective areas. This demonstrates how the concept of the Green Man has changed. With its reemergence in the 19th century, and its acceptance within a more "social" ethos, the image seemed to become more acceptable. It was more of a reminder of "olde England," or of a former world than of anything threatening. And as we have seen, the icon made its way into art, particularly comic book art, and seemed to have ensconced itself in modern culture. It has become more of a political force as well—lobbying for conservation and environmental issues. As ever, the Green Man remains with us, both as an icon and a perception down the ages.

Jack in the Green

The notion of the Green Man, then, contains many strands—psychological, mythological, historical, and traditional—all intertwined through each other. Perhaps this is the very reason why it has endured through the ages. However, untangling them all is a difficult task because the icon itself draws from many perspectives and cultures. It draws, for instance, from Christianity, but also from the Muslim and Hindu worlds of the East and from the vegetation gods of Africa and New Britain; it draws from literature that is both ancient and medieval and extends down into the modern idiom; it draws from art—from the stone bosses that glower down from the arches of churches and the signs hanging outside public houses. Indeed there is perhaps not a corner of popular culture that the image has not reached. Underlying the myth—though given the complexity of the icon, perhaps the word "myth" is the wrong one to use as it does not adequately address the subject—is the age-old relationship between Man and Nature and between life, death, and resurrection. There is also an acknowledgement of the passing of time, and of the coming and going of the seasons, and Mankind's attempts to come to terms with that. Here too is the linking of human life and the human experience to the changing world all around—the linkage between the passage of life, the turn of the seasons, and the hope of rebirth in either physical or spiritual form. This is the underpinning perspective, not only of Christianity, but of other religions as well.

In a very real and physical sense, the image of the Green Man addresses the mysteries of the cosmos and provides hope for the future. Because of this, belief in such an icon runs parallel with the world's great religions and perhaps satisfies the deepest human longing (to be an integral part of the cosmos) in a meaningful way. Perhaps too, that is the final and most enduring secret of the Green Man.

Further Reading

Kingsley Amis. *The Green Man.* (Jonathan Cape, 1969)

William Anderson and Clive Hicks. *Green Man.* (Compass Books, 1999)

M.D. Anderson. *Imagery of British Churches.* (John Murray, 1955)

Roger Anderson. *The Witch in the Wall.* (Allen and Unwin, 1977)

Kathleen Basford. *The Green Man.* (Boydell, 1978)

John Bate. *The Mysteries of Nature and Art.* (London, 1637)

J & C Bond. *Earth Rites, Fertility Practices in Pre-Industrial Britain.* (Granada, 1982)

R. Bernheimer. *Wild Men in the Middle Ages.* (Cambridge, Mass., 1952)

Katherine Briggs. *A Dictionary of Fairies.* (Penguin, 1977)

J. C. Cooper. *An Illustrated Encyclopaedia of Traditional Symbols.* (Thames and Hudson, 1978)

G. Chaney. *Images of the East.* (Centaur Press, 1951)

Bob Curran. *Encyclopaedia of Celtic Mythology.* (Appletree Press, 1999)

Brian Day. *A Chronicle of Folk Customs.* (Hamlyn, 1998)

Fran and Geoff Doel. *Robin Hood—Outlaw or Greenwood Myth.* (Tempus, 2000)

D.C. Fowler. *A Literary History of the Popular Ballad.* (North Carolina, 1968)

Sir James Frazer. *The Golden Bough.* (MacMillan, 1972)

Jeffrey Gantz (ed). *Early Irish Myth and Saga.* (Penguin, 1981)

F.H. Groom. *Gypsy Folk Tales.* (London, 1899)

Miranda Green. *Dictionary of Celtic Myth and Legend.* (Thames and Hudson, 1992)

Thirley Grundy. *The Green Man in Cumbria.* (Thumbprint, 2000)

Jeremy Hart. *The Green Man.* (Pitkin, 2001)

Clive Hicks. *The Green Man—A Field Guide.* (Compass, 2000)

Christina Hole. *A Dictionary of British Folk Customs.* (Paladin, 1978)

Ronald Hutton. *Stations of the Sun.* (OUP, 1996)

Roy Judge. *Jack in the Green.* (Boydell, 1979)

Maurice Keen. *Outlaws of Medieval England.* (Routledge & Kegan Paul, 1977)

Thomas Knightly. *The Customs and Ceremonies of Britain.* (Thames and Hudson, 1986)

Max Lehrs. *Late Gothic Engravings of Germany and the Netherlands.* (Dover Publications, 1969)

Bill Lewis. *Greenheart.* (Lazerwolf, 1996)

Caitlin Matthews. *Elements of the Celtic Tradition.* (Element, 1996)

F.M. McNeill. *The Silver Bough.* (William McLellan, 1959)

Margaret Murray. *The Divine King in England.* (Faber and Faber, 1954)

Margaret Murray. *The God of the Witches.* (OUP, 1952)

A. Nun. *The Fairy Mythology of Shakespeare.* (David Nutt, 1900)

Nigel Pennick. *Crossing the Borders.* (Coppal Bann Publishing, 1998)

Thomas Potter. *The Wild Hunt*. (Privately printed, 1932)

Lady Raglan. "The Green Man in Church Architecture." In *Folklore*. (1939) pp. 45–57

E. Rhys: Fairy Gold. *A Book of Old Fairy Tales*. (Dent)

D.W. Robertson. "Why the Devil Wears Green." In *Modern Language Notes*. (November, 1954)

Reginald Scot. *Discovery of Witchcraft*. (London, 1584)

Thomas Scott. *Travels in Tibet*. (Dent and Sons, 1927)

J.C. Smith. *A Guide to Church Woodcarvings*. (David and Charles, 1961)

Lewis Spence. *The Fairy Tradition in Britain*. (Rider, 1948)

W.E. Simeone. "The May Games and the Robin Hood Legend" in *Journal of American Folklore*. (1951) pp. 265–74

Philip Stubbes. *Anatomie of Abuses*. (1583)

P. Tilling. *Themes in Sir Gawain and the Green Knight*. (Cranagh Press, 1972)

Keith Thomas. *Witchcraft and the Decline of Magic*. (Penguin, 1978)

Ruth Tongue. *Forgotten Folk-Tales of the English Counties*. (Routledge and Kegan Paul, 1970)

Bob Trubshaw. "Facts and Fancies of the Foliate Face." In *At the Edge*. (1996) No. 4 pp. 25–28

Jacobus de Voragine. *The Golden Legend*. (Princeton, 1995)

Index

About the Author

Dr. Bob Curran was born and raised in a remote area of County Down, Northern Ireland. He has held a variety of jobs including gravedigger, lorry driver, professional musician, journalist, teacher, and lecturer. His rural background has given him an interest in folklore and mythology, and he has written extensively on these subjects in both books and journals. His books include *Vampires, Encyclopedia of the Undead, An Encyclopedia of Celtic Mythology, Bloody Irish*, and many others. Dr. Curran is also a historian and lectures extensively on culture and history. In this capacity, he sits on a number of cultural advisory bodies in Ireland, both North and South, and has produced several academic papers on various topics of cultural interest. He currently lives in the North of Ireland with his wife and young family.

Also by Bob Curran

Celtic Lore & Legend

Vampires

Encyclopedia of the Undead

Also Available from New Page Books

Mysteries of Druidry

Celtic Myth & Legend, Revised Ed.

Celtic Astrology